D0894843

A camping trip
to remember

When we'd eaten all we could eat, they sand-washed the plates and wiped out the skillet with a grease rag, then went to work setting up the tent. By the time the shadows started growing long, we had ourselves a genuine fishing camp on the banks of Wolf Creek.

Slim lit the kerosene lantern and chunked up the fire, and we watched the stars come out. Drover chased bugs and sparks from the fire, and Slim told some ghost stories. I could see the fire light dancing in Alfred's eyes. "See, Swim, isn't this fun?"

Slim poked at the fire with a stick. "Well, I don't want anyone to quote me on this, but it's turned out to be a pretty fine day. Fishing ain't as bad as I remembered. I think even your daddy might have enjoyed it."

The boy yawned. "Do you think it's going to rain?"

Slim laughed. "Not a chance. It ain't ever going to rain again. Let's turn in."

⌐ the

Lost Camp

John R. Erickson

Illustrations by Nicolette G. Earley
in the style of Gerald L. Holmes

Maverick Books, Inc.

MAVERICK BOOKS, INC.
Published by Maverick Books, Inc.
P.O. Box 549, Perryton, TX 79070
Phone: 806.435.7611
www.hankthecowdog.com

First published in the United States of America by Maverick Books, Inc. 2021.

1 3 5 7 9 10 8 6 4 2

LIBRARY OF CONGRESS CONTROL NUMBER: 2021948415

978-1-59188-177-3 (paperback); 978-1-59188-277-0 (hardcover)

Hank the Cowdog® is a registered trademark of John R. Erickson.

Printed in the United States of America

I dedicate this book to Dr. Blake DeWitt and the nursing staff at Ochiltree General Hospital. When I showed up at the emergency room at 10:30 at night with a rattlesnake bite, they took excellent care of me. I know it wasn't pleasant, treating a grumpy author-rancher, and I'm mighty grateful.

CONTENTS

CHAPTER ONE

Mud Daubers and Woodchucks

I t's me again, Hank the Cowdog. When we returned to Slim's house that hot afternoon in May, we weren't thinking about the Lost Camp or how it had gotten lost or even what it was, because at that point it didn't exist. When something doesn't exist, those of us in the Security Division don't waste time thinking about it.

We'll get to the camp business later on, so try to be patient. When we do, you'll probably get scared out of your wits. I mean, Little Alfred was there in the camp when the disaster came crashing…that's all I can reveal at this point, sorry.

Anyway, we had spent a hot, sweaty afternoon working on a stubborn windmill, and when we finally made it to Slim's shack on Wolf Creek, I could see the worries of the past six months etched onto his face: the dry winter without snow, a dry spring without rain or grass, relentless winds in March, hot dusty days, smoke from prairie fires, hungry cows, and brown everywhere.

Here we were in May, which was supposed to be the softest, sweetest, most fragrant month of the year, yet everything was drab and brown and smelled like dust.

Slim wasn't taking it well. Neither was I. Nobody on the ranch was taking it well. We'd been cheated out of springtime and we were permanently mad about it.

We'd all become grim and gripey and glum, and there was only one thing that could fix the problem: a good soaking rain. But Slim had already turned in his long-range weather prediction: rain was finished, we would never see another drop, the ranch would dry up and blow away.

That's where things stood when we pulled into Slim's place around seven o'clock in the evening of whatever day it was in May. It was hot and dry, of course, and Slim made the walk to the house bent over like an old man. Or a buzzard. Yes, he looked exactly like a buzzard, and he acted like one too: grim, glum, gloomy, gripey, and disagreeable. Every time his boot hit the ground, it kicked up a puff of dust.

When he reached the front porch, he stopped and looked up at the sky, a circle of bleached-out blue with a few thin stingy clouds. He shook his head and his scowl deepened. "There wouldn't be a raindrop in a whole trainload of them clouds."

So that was his prediction for the night: once again, no chance of rain, and that pretty muchly set the tone for the evening's entertainment. There wouldn't be any entertainment. We wouldn't be hunting mice with his slingshot or playing Slow Pitch Popcorn or Tug the Sock. We would all go to our separate corners of the house and suffer. At some point, weary from all the suffering, we would fall into a pitiful sleep and dream about dust and wind.

He didn't invite me and Drover into the house, which was fine with me. Who needed his gloom and doom? I could come up with plenty of it without his help. I staked out my spot on the porch and flopped down. Ouch. There was nothing soft or comfortable about that porch. I rose and tried to scratch it up into something better, but two-by-six lumber doesn't fluff up very well.

I happened to toss a glimpse at Drover. "What are you grinning about?"

"Oh, hi. Where'd you come from?"

"The same place you came from, Slim's pickup. We just got back from fixing a windmill in the middle pasture."

"I'll be derned, so did I. Maybe we were there together."

I heaved a sigh. "Drover, why were you grinning?"

"Gosh, was I grinning?"

"Of course you were grinning. Why would I ask why you were grinning unless you were grinning?"

"I wondered about that."

"If you'd been scowling, I would have asked why you were scowling. Why were you grinning?"

"Well, let me think." He rolled his eyes around

and pinched his face, while I drummed my toes and waited.

"Will you please hurry up?"

"I'm working on it."

At last, I'd had enough. I jacked myself up and marched over to him. "Look, pal, we haven't gotten any moisture in six months and the entire ranch is in a state of gloom. There is nothing to grin about, so why were you grinning?"

"If I told you, you'd laugh and make fun."

"That's a possibility. Out with it."

"Well...I thought...it might help."

I stared into the emptiness of his eyes. "What might help what? Grinning? You thought grinning might help it rain? Ha ha ha!"

"See? I knew you'd laugh and make fun."

"Of course. That is the craziest thing I ever heard. Why do I bother talking to you?" I returned to my spot on the porch, did the Three Turns Maneuver, and flopped down. A minute slid by. I got up and went back to him. "Okay, I'm curious. How could grinning help?"

"Promise you won't make fun again?"

"No promises. Talk, out with it."

"Well, gloom doesn't seem to be working."

"Drover, nobody expects gloom to produce rain."

"Then what's the point?"

I began pacing, as I often do when I'm speaking to a class of birdbrains. "The point is that we must be gloomy because *our people are gloomy*. It's part of our jog as daubs."

"What's a daub?"

"A daub is lump of clay. Your mud daubers are a variety of wasp and they build nests out of daubs of clay."

"I'll be derned."

"That's why we call them mud daubers, don't you see."

"Yeah, and it's easier to say 'mud daubers' than 'wasps.'"

"Hm, I hadn't thought of that. It's a tough word, isn't it? Wass-puh-suss."

"Yeah, it makes you hiss when you say it. Wasp-pss-pss-pss."

"Right, and it sounds silly. Good observation."

"Thanks. But where would a mud dauber find mud in a drought?"

I stopped pacing. "I'd never thought about it. If there's no mud, how can a mud dauber daub mud?"

"Yeah, and how can a woodchuck chuck wood? I've always wondered about that too."

I studied the runt. "Drover, for once in your life, you seem to have come to class prepared. This is a good discussion and all at once I'm wondering…is there a song in this?"

His face went blank. "A song? How could there be a song about wasps and woodchucks?"

"I admit that it won't be easy, but maybe… wait. I'm beginning to hear notes and words, the very things that songs are made of. I think we can do this. We'll start with a basic waltz rhythm: 1-2-3, 1-2-3, 1-2-3-4-5-6."

"I can't count that high."

"Please hush. On top of the rhythm, we'll add poetic words and four-part harmony."

"I can't do four-part harmony."

"Then I'll do it by myself. Listen to this."

The Wasp Song

Wasp-pss-pss, Wasp-pss-pss, Wasp-pss-pss-pss.

Mud-daub-ers, Mud-daub-ers, Mud-daub-er-ers.

Wood-chuck-chucks, Wood-chuck-chucks,
Wood-chuck-chuck-chucks.

I finished the song and turned back to Drover. "Well, what do you think?"

His face had gone from blank to blanker. "I don't get it."

"Drover, it's a song. There's nothing to get.

You either like it or you don't."

"It doesn't make sense. What do woodchucks have to do with wasps and mud?"

I resumed my pacing. "Okay, I'll try to explain. In the song, we've got two different themes going at the same time. On the one hand, we have woodchucks and on the other, we have mud daubers. And they're very different."

"Yeah, woodchucks have buck teeth."

"Exactly, and mud daubers have no teeth at all. That's a huge difference. Furthermore, your woodchucks don't daub mud and your mud daubers don't chuck wood, which goes to prove..." I stopped pacing and tried to collect my thoughts. "How did we get on the subject of woodchucks?"

"Well, you were talking about mud daubers and they turned into woodchucks, and then you wrote a song."

"Yes, well, that's strange, because we don't even have woodchucks in Texas."

"Gosh, where do they live?"

"I have no idea. I've never seen one, so it seems odd that we'd be talking about them and that brings up another question. Why were we talking about mud daubers?"

"Let me think here." There was a long moment of silence and I could see that he was working on it. "Wait, I've got it. You said that being gloomy is part of our jog as daubs, and I asked you what a daub was."

I stared at the runt. *Our jog as daubs?* Was this some kind of clue I had missed, an important detail that would send the Security Division plunging into a new investigation and possibly shed some light on the mysterious Lost Camp which didn't exist at that point?

To find out, you'll have to keep reading. This is something we need to check out.

CHAPTER TWO

The Impossible Happens

I guess you're still with me. Good. For several minutes, I wrestled with Drover's mysterious statement, and the longer I pondered it, the more I felt my temper rising. "Number one, I didn't say it's our jog as daubs. I said it's our JOB AS DOGS."

"Maybe you said it wrong."

"Maybe your ears need cleaning. Open your mouth and say 'ahh.'"

He opened his mouth. "Ahhhhh."

I peered inside. "Your ears are filthy. No wonder you're going deaf. Close your mouth. Number two, you have succeeded in drawing me into a ridiculous discussion about bugs and woodchucks, and do you know why?"

"No, why?"

I stuck my nose in his face. "Because you never come to class prepared, that's why. You just sit there like a toad stool and babble nonsense. You've wasted valuable time and caused me to compose a ridiculous song, and this will go into my gradebook. For that miserable performance, you will get three Flunk Marks."

"Oh darn."

"Please don't curse and swear in class."

"Oh booger."

"That's gross."

"Oh fizzle."

"That's better. Number four…"

"I think it's number three."

"Please hush. Number five, the whole point of this lecture was that you were grinning in a No Grin Period. During a drought, dogs should be grim and not grin."

"Well, I only missed it by one letter."

"Drover, there's only one letter's difference between 'foot' and 'food.' Get that letter wrong and you'll eat your foot at Scrap Time. How would you like that? Is that what you want to do with your life, eat your own foot?"

His head sank. "I'm so confused! I don't want to eat my foot and I don't care about woodchucks."

"Then you're going to have to make some

changes in your life, and you should start by cleaning out your ears."

He sniffled. "All I said was that if gloom can't make it rain, why not try something else?"

I tried to soften my approach. I didn't want to make him cry. "Drover, listen to me. Dogs and cowboys have gone through many droughts together and we've always responded with gloom. Now, all at once, you want to smash tradition and go skipping off into an entirely new and unknown direction—grinning?"

"Well, I don't see how it could hurt to try."

I heaved a groan, I mean, he was wearing me out. "All right, have it your way. Go ahead, be a rebel and grin, but I warn you. If the drought continues, we will hold you irresponsible."

"Yeah, but what if it rains?"

I laughed. "If it rains, pigs will wear lipstick and you'll get a big promotion."

I left the little goofball, returned to my spot on the porch, did a quick TTM (Three Turns Maneuver), and flopped down...ouch...on solid planks that had gotten even solider and plankier than before.

I had wasted fifteen minutes of my life, talking to a dunce and trying to raise his IQ a few points. Instead, he had lowered mine at least fifty points and maybe a hundred. Have you ever heard such a weird conversation? Not me, and I'd been though some doozies with the same guy.

Grinning up a rain. That was weird beyond weird, weird times ten, and I had no idea how he had derailed my lecture and sent my whole train of thought over the cliff, into a pit full of mud daubers and woodchucks.

It was incredible. No, it was worse than that. It was scary that one little mutt could inflict so much damage to a normal, rational conversation, but he does this to me all the time. I start off talking about something sane and normal, and end up talking about purple giraffes and dancing rutabagas.

I'll say no more about it, except to say one more thing about it. It's crazy and embarrassing, and it's no way to run a Security Division. The success and survival of this ranch depend on a Security Division whose officers and men have enough sense to pour sand out of a boot. Drover couldn't pour sand out of a sand box. He couldn't find a grain of sand in the Sahara Desert or a boot on Boot Hill.

I should have fired him years ago, but I'm too nice. Good old easy-going Hank. And look what it got me. My assistant was sitting like a little statue on the edge of the porch, staring up at a

14

sky that didn't have one cloud in it, and grinning like a lunatic.

I should have left it alone, but I just couldn't. "Hey Drover, how's that rain coming along?"

"Oh, I'm still working on it."

"Well, don't get discouraged. The world can always use another dumb idea."

"Yeah, and don't forget the Wise Old Saying: 'If at first you don't succeed, try, try and grin.' That's what I'm doing and I think it might work."

I had to stuff a cork into the bottle of my laughter. "I bet it will, son, just keep it up."

"Gosh, thanks. I was afraid you might think it was silly."

"Oh no, not silly. Courageous. Every bonehead idea is just waiting for some quiet genius to prove that it's a bonehead idea."

"That makes me feel better, thanks."

"Glad to help out. Listen, when you get that rain grinned up, give me a shout. I don't want to miss a single drop."

"Okay, but it might take a while. Don't wait up."

"All right, if you think you can handle it, I'll grab a few Z's. Nighty hee hee."

"What?"

"I said nighty night. Go get 'em, soldier!"

"Got it, thanks again."

I almost damaged my innards, trying to keep from laughing. Grinning up a rain! I closed my eyes and surrendered myself to the…but you know what? I couldn't sleep. No kidding. My conscience was chewing away on my…something. I felt like a rat, laughing at a poor little guy who, in his own weird way, was flying to herp the runch out of a snork…trying to help the ranch out of a drought, let us say.

No, I just couldn't sneep honking donkey donut in the fiddling shish kabob's royal highness…zzzzzz…fuzzy wuzzy wasn't fuzzy, wuzzy? Blop mop buffering bananas…zzzzzzzz.

"Hank, you'd better wake up!"

"I'm snot asneep."

"Yeah, you are and you need to see this. It's raining!"

Huh?

I staggered to someone's feet, okay, maybe they were mine, and pried open two eyelids, also mine, and saw…who was that guy? And what was the flash of light? I blinked my eyes and reached for the mustard. "Where is my hot dog and who are you?"

"Well, there's not a hot dog, but I'm Drover. Remember me?"

"No. Wait. Are you a hot dog?"

"No, I'm just normal. We're on Slim's porch

and you were asleep."

"That's impossible. I wasn't even here. How can I conduct this symphony if nobody brings me the mustard?" I blinked again and noticed...well, some kind of face with one eye and two noses...no, wait, two eyes and one nose. "You look like Drover."

"Thanks. You look like Hank and it looks like rain."

"How can I look like rain? I'm not even a cloud and it hasn't rained in years."

"Well, it's raining now."

"That's impossible. We already know that this ranch is unrainable and..." I heard a sound behind me, perhaps a door opening, a secret door that led to some dark secret place. I whirled around and fired off a Quick Bark. In these situations, we never know what might be coming, don't you see, so a QB is the safe call.

"Hank, dry up."

Did you hear that? Maybe not, because you weren't there, but I heard it and the owner of the voice *knew my name*. Maybe they'd hacked into our systems and had us surrounded!

I whirled back to the mutt beside me. "Where are we?"

"Slim's house, on the porch."

"Who is that guy?"

"Slim Chance."

"Never heard of him, but maybe this is his house."

"That's what I said."

"What are those flashing lights?"

"Lightning. It's raining."

"Raining! Why wasn't I informed?"

"Well, I tried but you were zonked out."

"I was not zonked out! How can I command a battleship when my crew is spreading lies and hiding information?" In a flash of light, I saw the strange man again. "Roy, that man is almost naked."

"Yeah, he sleeps in his drawers and a T-shirt. And my name's Drover, not Roy."

"I don't care what name you're using. I smell something wet in the air. Is the ship taking on water?"

"No, it's raining."

"Raining! Why doesn't anyone tell me these things?"

"Well, I tried about five times."

At that very moment, the naked man let out a yell. "Holy cow, IT'S RAINING!"

I turned back to Roy...Drover, whatever he called himself. "He says it's raining."

"Duh."

"Don't duh me, you insolent little whicker-snicker, or I'll have you tossed in the brig!"

The naked man...Slim, I guess it was...stepped out on the porch and held both hands up in the air. "Rain, by grabs, real honest-to-Betsy rain!" He stepped off the porch and tip-toed across the yard to the fence. There, he lifted something out of a metal frame, a kind of glass tube, and brought it up to his face, then let out a crazy laugh and yelled, "Yee-HA! Seventy hundredths!" Then he skipped back to the house and stood under a stream of water that was pouring off the roof.

And that's how the mystery began on a dark night, with a naked man standing out in the rain. Actually, he wasn't totally naked. He wore a T-shirt and boxer shorts, but he was the nakedest man I'd ever seen standing out in the rain. I mean, that's not something we'd seen before on my ranch.

You have to admit it sounds pretty creepy.

CHAPTER THREE

An Intruder in the Night

I turned to the dog next to me. "What's wrong with him?

"Well, it's raining and I guess he's happy."

"It's raining? Here? That's impossible!" He shrugged. "Don't shrug when I talk to you! Stand up straight and deliver crisp answers to your commanding officer. How could it be raining?"

"Well, I've been out here all night, trying to grin up a rain, and it finally worked. Hee hee. Are you proud of me?"

For a moment, I was speechless. "We'll deal with you later. Right now, I've got a rain to take care of. Go to your room."

"I don't have a room. This is the porch."

"Don't argue with me. Find a room and make

yourself useful." A stream of light was coming from inside the house and lit up his face. "Wait a second, you're Drover, right?" I blinked my eyes and tried to clear the fog out of my bog. "I must have dozed off."

"Yeah, about five hours ago."

"Drover, I'd be grateful if you'd forget this ever happened. If word leaked out, it could create rumors and gossip. I'm sure you understand. Now, what is that man doing, standing out there in the rain?"

"Well, he's standing out there in the rain, I guess."

"Has he ever done this before?"

"Not that I know of."

"Hmm. Don't go to your room just yet. We need to check this out and I might need backup."

This situation raised a lot of unanswered eyebrows. A lot of unanswered *questions*, it should be, and come to think of it, *all* questions are unanswered when they come into this world. See, a question that already has an answer isn't a question any more. Here, let's go to the blackboard and write it out in a mathematical equation. Check this out:

-1 = Q = a question

+1 = A = an answer

A + Q = 0 because +1 + -1 = 0

In other words, when a question collides with an answer, the question explodes into tiny particles that are gobbled up by bats and toads. Wow, is this cool or what? I get a kick out of digging deep into things with heavy duty math, and it's good for the kids too. They need to exercise their little minds and they need to know that all questions are unanswered. That kind of information can come in very handy.

Now, where were we? Does anyone remember what we were talking about? Hmm. Let's see... Drover and I were out on Slim's porch and...I had taken a short nap, remember? A very short nap, just a few minutes, because, well, this job is a dog-killer and we have to grab sleep whenever we can, and somehow we got on the subject of unanswered questions.

I'm still drawing a blank and that's...wait! There was this naked man, standing out in the rain, only he wasn't exactly naked but pretty close, and his name was Slim Chance. Remember?

Now we're cooking, and it raised a bunch of questions, is the whole point, such as, "What on earth was he doing, standing out in the rain in the middle of the night in his underwear?" It was one of the biggest unanswered questions I had encountered in my whole career, and before my very eyes, as I watched, it became even more unanswered.

He'd been standing under a stream of water that was pouring off the roof, remember? Well, he got soaked, and then…you might not believe this part…and then he laid down in the puddle below the porch and ROLLED AROUND in it, splashing and laughing like a crazy person!

I turned to Drover. "I'm not believing this."

"Yeah, me neither. I guess all those months without rain made him a little daffy."

"I guess they did. It's kind of shocking."

"Yeah. Cowboys."

"Exactly. I doubt that there's another group of humans who would behave that way." We continued watching this odd display. "But you know what? It's the sort of thing a dog might enjoy doing."

"Not me. I hate water."

"Oh, come on, Drover. Don't you think it might be fun to romp around in a puddle? It would give us a chance to spend some Quality Time with our cowboy. It would be a bonding experience."

"I'll bond with the porch. Water's too wet for me."

"Drover, water is supposed to be wet."

"Yeah, and I'm supposed to be dry."

"Oh brother. Well, I'm going to join my cowboy

and celebrate the end of a long, painful dry spell. You can sit on the porch and snap at flies."

"Fine with me."

What a weird little mutt. I left him there with all his dry hairs, and dived off the porch, right into the muddle of Slum's piddle...right into the middle of Slim's puddle, shall we say. I made a big splash and he was surprised.

"Good honk! Well, hi Hankie, welcome to the new world! What do you think of this rain?"

Great stuff, very refreshing after months of dust.

"This is the best rain I ever saw in my whole

life! Seventy hundredths! I love it, can't believe it, thought it was never going to rain again, but it did and thank you, Lord!"

He whooped and hollered, laughed and squealed and splashed like a little kid, then grabbed me around the middle and we rolled around in the mud and water. It was the kind of spontaneous event that happens only once or twice in a lifetime, a cowboy and his dog lost in the pure wonder of rain and clean air and friendship.

It was the sort of thing neither of us would have done in public. See, most people, and even some dogs, would have thought it was pretty strange, but we were alone on the ranch, out in the middle of nowhere and...

Neither of us saw the car pull up in front of the house, I mean, we were pretty busy, and neither of us saw the headlights or heard a car door slam or anything, until Slim noticed the beam of a flashlight...on us.

He froze. So did I.

The rain had quit. In the beam of the flashlight, Slim appeared to be...well, not quite human, I mean, we're talking about some kind of Mud Monster from another planet. I hardly recognized him—two eyes staring out of a mask of brown goo and hair that looked like a pile of moss.

Maybe I should have barked, but by then, I was curious to know who was behind the flashlight. I could see pant legs and boots, and that was about it. Whoever it was had two legs and two feet. Then we heard a voice.

"Your neighbors called and said there were a couple of drunks having a party."

Slim heaved a sigh, pushed me away, sat up, and wrapped his arms around his knees. "Bobby, I've told you this before. *You ain't funny*."

Wait, hold everything! Did you hear that? "Bobby." It was Chief Deputy Bobby Kile, and I knew the guy.

He spoke. "I'm just trying to do my job as an officer of the law."

"No, I'm serious. You ain't funny but you keep trying to be."

A sprig of sunlight popped over the horizon and we could see a big grin on the deputy's face. He was enjoying this. He switched off the flashlight. Slim pushed himself to his feet and went to the hydrant on the north side of the house, turned it on and washed most of the mud off his carcass.

He came back to the porch and waved a bony finger in the air. "And I'll tell you something else. It strikes me as creepy that you always show up exactly when I don't want to see anyone. There are times when you ought to keep your big nose out of other peoples' business."

We heard a snort of laughter. "Should I ask what's going on here?"

"Well, it rained."

"Yes?"

"It rained after six months of stinking drought and I decided to celebrate. I got out of bed and jumped in a puddle with my dog. If it looks dumb, I don't care. It's my rain and I can do what I want with it. It's just a shame the citizens of this county can't celebrate a blessed event without some busybody from the sheriff's department showing up to ruin it."

"How much did you get?"

"Seventy hundredths, the best rain I've seen in my whole life."

"That's good. Boy, this old country sure needed it."

"We needed more but it's a good start on spring grass." Slim narrowed his eyes. "Now, tell me the truth. What in the cat hair are you doing out here, creeping around in the dark?"

"I got called out. Lighting struck an oil field tank battery, blew it a hundred feet and started a fire, but the rain put it out. I was in your neighborhood and thought I'd stop by and say hello. I didn't realize that you and Hank would be taking a swim."

"I guess you should have called first."

"You got any coffee?"

"No. I've been busy. Go find your own coffee."

The deputy smiled. "Boy, you're all sweetness and light in the morning."

"Bobby, come back some time when you're invited and I'll try to be more pleasant."

"What are you going to do the rest of the day?"

"I don't know. When I figure it out, I'll send you a post card."

"Well, you might want to take a bath. Good luck and congratulations on the rain." He turned and walked toward his squad car.

Slim yelled, "Hey, did you get any rain at your place?"

"Yeah, I checked the gauge before I left the house."

"How much?"

"Two and a half inches."

He got into the car and drove away.

The One-Puddle
Rain

I happened to be looking at Slim when he heard Deputy Kile's rainfall report. His eyes bugged out and his jaw dropped. He looked as though he'd been slugged in the gut. Then he started getting mad. Oh my, did he get mad! What happened next was pretty strange, so hang on.

He stomped across the yard on his skinny pipe-cleaner mayonnaise-colored legs, snatched the rain gauge out of its holder, glared at it with blazing eyes, and flung the water out of it. "Stupid rain gauge!" He swung his glare up to the clouds, which were breaking up and moving away. He shook his fist at them. "Y'all are pitiful! If that's the best you can do, you ought to go find another job!"

Then he…this was pretty crazy…he threw the rain gauge all the way to the saddle shed and came storming back to the porch, and fellers, the look on his face chilled my gizzard. We're talking about Halloween. Drover saw it too and vanished around the south side of the house.

I swallowed hard and switched my tail over to Puzzled But Caring Wags, held my position on the porch and hoped that, well, maybe my presence would be some comfort to him in this dark moment.

To be honest, I wasn't sure why the moment had become so dark. Ten minutes ago, he and I had been rolling around in a mud puddle, filled with joy and happiness, a cowboy and his dog celebrating a new day and a good life and a beautiful rain…and now, this.

It didn't make sense, but we dogs don't get paid to understand Life and all its many so-forths. We get paid to BE THERE when they need us, and ask no questions, and by George I was there, on duty and ready to serve.

He came tromping up the stops and stepped. He came tromping up the steps and stopped, there we go, and looked down at me. I switched the tail over to Slow Wags that said, "Boy, that was fun, rolling around in a mudhole with you. Hanging out with cowboys can be pretty exciting."

Would those words bring him some comfort? The angry look on his face didn't soften and at last he spoke. "He got two and a half inches of rain! It makes me want to throw up."

Then he was gone, into the house, maybe to take a bath. He wasn't one to over-bathe, but on this occasion, he needed it. He had washed off the worst of the mud with the water hose, but he still had brown streaks on his face and across his back. And his hair still looked like something you might find washed up on a beach.

I wasn't able to help him with his bath because he didn't invite me inside. He would have to do it on his own and maybe he wouldn't mess anything up.

Maybe you think there's no way a grown man could mess up taking a bath, but you'd be wrong. Remember the time he got his big toe stuck in the water spigot? That was incredible. The Security Division had let him take a bath without the supervision of a qualified dog and that's what we got, a cowboy with his big toe hung in a bathtub water spigot.

Oh well, he was on his own today and we could only hope that he didn't do anything crazy in the tub.

I sat on the porch and watched the sun come over the horizon and buzzards flapping low in the sky. We see them doing this in the early morning hours, don't you know, leaving the tree where they roost at night and skimming along at a low altitude.

I heard a swishing sound behind me and, just for a second, thought it might be a buzzard. I whirled to the right and saw a nose and then a face, peeking around the corner of the house. Then a voice said, "Is it safe to come out?" It was Drover, of course.

"All clear, come on out."

He crept out and came over to me, casting worried glances all around. "Who was that guy who was yelling and throwing things?"

"That was Slim. He had a little temper tantrum."

"It didn't look so little to me. What did you do this time?"

"It saddens me that you would put it that way. For your information, I had nothing to do with it."

"That's weird."

"But since you asked, we might as well get this over with."

"Get what over with?"

"Sit down in the witness chair. Court is now in session and you are under oath." He sat down and I began pacing, as I often do when I'm grilling a witness. "Tell this court what you were doing on the porch between sundown and first light."

"Well, let me think here. I was sitting."

"Yes, and what else?"

"Well, I scratched a couple of times. And chased a June bug and listened to you making a bunch of noise in your sleep."

"Objection! The witness is dabbling in hearsay and gossip. Sustained." I marched over to him and glared into his eyes. "There was more going on, wasn't there? Isn't it true, Drover, that you were sitting on the porch and *grinning*?"

"Well…"

"Tell this court why you were grinning."

His face melted into a silly grin. "Oh yeah, I almost forgot. I was trying to grin up a rain. And it worked!"

I was really stalking him now. "So you admit that you grinned up the rain?"

"Oh yeah, and you didn't think I could do it." He actually stuck out his tongue at me. "So there, hee hee!"

"Drover, you're in a court of law. Please refrain from childish displays. Your Honor, let the record state that the witness stuck out his tongue at the prosecutor."

"Well, it's true. You didn't think I could grin up a rain."

"Please hush. So you're telling this court that you willfully and knowingly grinned up a rain.

Do you happen to remember how much rain you grinned up?"

"Well, let me think here." He squinted one eye and rolled the other one around. "I think Slim said...seven hundred thousand."

"That's incorrect. He checked the rain gauge and reported that it contained seventy hundredths of an inch of rain."

"Maybe that was it."

I whirled around and prepared to spring the trap. "Drover, did it ever occur to you that seventy hundredths was a pitiful amount of rain?"

"Not really."

"Not really? Is that all you can say?"

"Well, it made a nice puddle."

"Poor Slim had endured six months of crushing drought and he got *one mud puddle* as a reward? Does that sound fair and just?"

His head began to sink. "Well, he played in it, and so did you."

"Yes, but did it ever occur to you that Chief Deputy Kile had received *two and a half inches of rain*, more than three times the amount you grinned up for Slim? How many mud puddles did Deputy Kile get?"

He shook his head and seemed close to tears. "I don't know."

"You don't know or you don't care? Drover, that pitiful little rain you grinned up has ruined Slim's day. It has left him crushed and angry. He threw his rain gauge all the way down to the saddle shed and he's been forced to take a bath on a weekday. He's a broken man."

His lip trembled. "I was just trying to help."

"The defendant will rise."

"Is that me?"

"Yes, on your feet, and don't scratch." He stood up. "This court finds you guilty of grinning up a rain that was only one-third as big as Deputy Kile's. You will stand with your nose in the corner for five minutes."

His face collapsed. "You said I would get a promotion."

"Right, this is it."

"Three whole minutes?"

"Yes, three whole minutes. March to the dungeon and begin your sentence. And don't even think about cheating."

"How'd you know?"

"Because I know you've picked up sneaky tricks from the cat."

"Oh darn."

"And I've already warned you about naughty language."

"Oh piffle piddle poodle."

I ignored his trash-talk. He dragged himself to the southwest corner of the porch and deposited his nose about fifteen inches above the floor. "Higher."

"It hurts my neck."

"Nobody cares. I'm starting the timer."

"Two whole minutes?"

"Absolutely."

I've said this before but I'll say it again. I hate being hard on the men, but if we don't set rules and standards and impose justice, everything will go to pot around here. If the runt was going to grin up a rain, he needed to grin up one that would beat Deputy Kile and all the other neighbors.

Don't forget that rainfall is the most important ingredient in ranch management. Everything else is in a tie for last place. One-puddle rains won't cut it on this outfit. That duck won't hunt.

CHAPTER FIVE

Drover Goes To Jail

D rover had gotten a fair trial and I wanted to be sure he served every second of his Nose Time. Hencely, I kept a close eye on the timer, and there would be no talk of early parole or time off for good behavior. He'd made such a big deal out of grinning up the rain, he needed to pay the pauper.

Pay the plumber.

He needed to pay whoever gets paid in these legal proceedings. The piper, there we go. He needed to pay the piper.

You might be wondering if he actually *did* grin up the rain. I wondered about that too. There are no scientific studies that suggest a direct link between a stub-tailed mutt, grinning on the porch of a cowboy's shack, and a weather system that produces rain, but we can't ignore a pretty impressive line of evidence. Here, let's call up a slide. Pay attention to the screen.

- The defendant said he was going to grin up a rain.
- Defendant stayed up most of the night, grinning at the clouds.
- Shortly before daylight, those clouds released rain.

What can you say? It's not air-tight, irreguffable proof that he did it, and science needs to do a lot more work on this, but it makes a pretty strong argument that *something* happened, and it was enough to get him thrown in jail for malpractice. I mean, if you're going to blab it around that you're a hot-shot rainmaker, you'd better be sure that Slim gets more water in his rain gauge than Deputy Kile gets in his. That's just the way the game is played around here.

See, Slim and Deputy Kile had a long-running, serious competition going on, a kind of Battle of the Rain Gauges. I happened to know that one time, after a little summer shower, Slim slipped over to the deputy's place in the country and filled his gauge to the five-inch mark.

Naturally, the deputy was excited and called it in to the local radio station, where it became big news for about thirty minutes, until the fraud was exposed.

A few months later, we got a nice shower at the ranch and when we got back to Slim's place, he couldn't wait to check his gauge. He was surprised to find three inches of *milk* in the tube, with a Cheerio floating around on top. He got a good chuckle out of that one, and said, "Old Bobby can be dangerous."

But back to Drover's jail time. I had every reason to think that he would try to cheat his way into an early release. See, he had a history hanging out with bad company—the local cat—and when the chips were down, we had to assume that his chips would be trying to cheat.

When dogs hang out with cats, even good dogs can get corrupted. It's sad to say and sadder to see, but I've seen that scene before. Wait a second, that has the bounce of a poem. Let's work on that. Check this out:

> *It's sad to say and sadder to see, I've seen*
> *this scene before.*
> *It seems the scene is rarely seen but rotten*
> *to the core.*
> *How could it be any other way when you*
> *factor in the fact*
> *It involves a rotten character, Sally May's*
> *despicable cat.*

Wow, that came out pretty well, don't you think? Thanks, I agree. I get a kick out of stringing words together and making them dance and rhyme. Show me another dog who can go from big-time litigation to scientific weather studies to crinimal investigations, and then top it off with an awesome poem. I'm not one to call attention to myself, but wow.

Anyway, I'd seen the scene before. Cats cheat. They love to cheat. They do it as a profession. They do it as a hobby. They would rather cheat than eat ice cream.

So, yes, I made double-sure the runt didn't cheat his way out of jail. I hawked him like a watch but had to listen to him moan and whine. "Hank, there's a spider in this corner!"

"Well, you won't get lonely."

"What if he bites me?"

"Bite him back."

"Yeah, but what if it's a black widow?

"Widow snickle cucumber pickle."

"If they bite you on the nose, your nose falls off."

"Nosey posey puddin' and pie."

"Are you asleep?"

"Sleepy weepy foggy fiddle."

"Hee hee. Hank? HANK!"

"Huh? What?"

"My time's up."

I blinked my eyes. "Already?"

"Yeah, it was awful. I hated it, two whole hours, and my neck's killing me."

"You were locked up for two hours? I wonder if I might have dozed off."

"Oh surely not."

I yawned. "Well, I hope you learned a lesson from this experience."

"Oh yeah, I learned a whole bunch." He came skipping out of his cell, wearing a big grin.

"Would you like to tell us what you learned?"

"Oh, I'd better not. Besides, you already know everything."

"Hmm, good point. There's no sense in rehashing old hash."

"Boy, I love hash."

"Me too. Slim used to open a can of hash every now and then, but I guess it got too expensive and he switched to canned mackerel."

"Yeah, and boiled turkey necks."

"The turkey necks are pretty good, but that mackerel is bad stuff."

"Boy, I'm starved."

"Me too. All at once, I'm thinking about food."

"I'll be derned. Me too. I wonder what brought it on."

"Life, Drover. Food is a very important part of Life and I wonder if there's any chance of getting some breakfast around here. I'd even take some mackerel. Maybe you could scratch on the screen door and we could check things out."

"Oh sure, I'd be glad to." He took three steps toward the door and went down like a sack of cement. "Oh darn, this old leg just went out on me!"

"Drover, I hope this isn't one of your hypocardiac events."

"Oh no, it's the real thing this time. Oh, the pain! I must have strained my neck in jail."

"Your neck is a long way from your leg."

"Yeah, but they're both connected to the bogus nerve."

"I guess that's true. Okay, get out of the way and I'll do the scratching."

He dragged his potsrate body out of my path and I had to admit that he looked pretty crippled up. Maybe two hours of Nose Time had been too much for his little body. I hate to be severe with the men...we've already covered that, but the point is that at the top of the mountaintop of the mountain, where I operate every day, life is seldom easy or pleasant.

I stepped around the runt and marched over

to the screen door. I knew that putting the Screen Scratching Protocol into action would involve certain risks, but our troops were starving. Sometimes we have to step up and take chances. I would have preferred risking Drover, but it appeared that he was out of action.

I lifted my right paw, placed it on the screen, applied pressure, and made a downward sweep. SKRITCH! I waited and listened. I could hear the thump of feet inside the house. That would be Slim and he was out of the tub. Good. He hadn't drowned or gotten his toe hung in the spigot.

I froze in place and stared at the door, waiting for it to open. It didn't open and needed another treatment. "Drover, how's the leg doing?"

"Terrible pain."

"Maybe a little exercise…"

"Oh my leg!"

I took a big breath of air and initiated the program again, a little harder this time. SCRITCH! I cocked my ear and listened. Ah, footsteps, and they were coming this way. The door opened and there stood Slim. I squeezed up a big smile and…

SPLAT!

…got a pan of cold water right in the face.

"Quit scratching on my screen door, you birdbrain!" The door slammed shut. Dripping water and blinking drips, I returned to the spot Drover was occupying.

He stared at me. "How'd it go?"

"How do you suppose it went?"

"Not so well. I guess it means no breakfast."

"That's one of the things it means. The other thing it means is that you get five Chicken Marks and it will go into my report."

"Gosh, what did I do?"

I bored into him with two drill-bit eyes. "I saw that little grin just now. You thought it was funny that I got sloshed. Go ahead and admit it."

"Oh no, I would never hee hee."

"What?"

"I said, I would tee hee never tee hee over such a thing."

"I'm almost sure I saw you grinning."

His eyes popped open. "Oh, that. Yeah, I was trying to grin up another rain."

"Are you being sincere?"

"Oh yes. But it didn't work and now I'm all discouraged."

I laid a paw on his shoulder. "Don't let it get you down, son. Sometimes we just have to trudge on. And we'll forget about those Chicken Marks."

"Gosh, thanks."

"How's the leg?"

He stood up, put some weight on the leg, and hobbled a few steps. "You know, I think it's doing a little better. At least I can limp on it now."

"Good, good. That bogus nerve can cause a lot of..."

At that moment, I heard a sound behind me, whirled around, and saw Slim coming out the door. He was dressed for a day's work and still wore a sour expression on his face.

I turned to my assistant. "Psst, he needs a boost. Let's try Happy Dog."

"Got it."

We turned to face him and launched the Happy Dog Presentation: a friendly show of teeth, sparkling eyes, ears that were up and alert, and tails that seemed to be wagging a song of pure happiness. Drover's wags weren't all that impressive, for obvious reasons, but he put his little heart and stub tail into the program.

Slim walked right past us and mumbled, "Meatheads."

Big Plans

That hurt, I mean it really hurt. We don't always expect to get a bonus for the many things we do around here, but for crying out loud! All that work and preparation, just for him, and all we got was "meathead."

For a moment, I thought Drover might burst into tears. "He hates us!"

"No, he doesn't. He hated the rain."

"I thought he loved the rain."

"Well, he did."

"Y'all swam around in the puddle and had fun, and he was in his shorts and looked like a Mud Monster."

"Drover, I know all that. It was a nice little rain and he enjoyed it, but then he found out that

Deputy Kile's rain was better and, well, it shattered his spirit." I paced a few steps away. "Look, don't ask me to explain these people. They're hard to figure out. We dogs are easy because we're logical, reasonable, kind, gentle, considerate, reasonable, and logical."

He sniffled. "You're right. I hadn't thought of that."

"Slim is doing the best he can. He's just a quart low in certain areas. We have to be patient and hope that, one of these days, maybe he'll learn from his dogs."

"Yeah, we can try to be good examples."

"Exactly my point, and it might be the most important part of our job. Do you know who's the real meathead on this ranch?"

"Well, that's a toughie."

"Slim, and maybe he can't help it. Now, let's stick with our guy and see if we can bring him around. He's having a bad day."

Pretty touching, huh? You bet. Our people have no idea how hard we work to bring them a few shreds of hope and happiness.

Slim slouched his way to the pickup. He opened the door and glanced around. Do you see the meaning of this? It meant that, even though the Rain Disaster had turned his heart into petrified wood, he was looking to see if we dogs still cared about him.

It wasn't much of a gesture—crumbs, in fact—but it brought a little ray of sunshine into our lives, enough to keep us going. I turned back to Drover and gave him a wink.

It went right past him. "Something's wrong with your eye."

"Nothing's wrong with my eye. I winked to let you know...just skip it. The point is that Slim is waiting for us to load into the pickup,"

"I thought we were meatheads."

"Drover, some parts of this life are very subtle and you have to pay attention. Are you going on this mission or staying on the porch?"

He glanced around. "Oh, there's too many spiders on the porch and I'm scared of spiders."

"All right, then, let's load up!"

We dived off the porch, grabbed a gear, and went streaking to the pickup. I got there first, of course, and throttled down to a stop. Slim gave me a grumpy look and said, "Ya'll don't deserve to ride up in first-class."

Too bad. I dived into the cab and took my position at the shotgun-side window. Drover took three stabs at climbing inside and Slim finally had to give him a boost. And then—this was the non-surprise of the year—and then he gave me a whimpering look and said, "I never get to ride Shotgun."

We had gone over this so many times in the past, I didn't bother to list the fifteen good reasons why we couldn't allow him to ride Shotgun. I ignored him and said nothing. Okay, I said something: "Tough toenails."

The ride to headquarters was very solemn, very quiet. Slim had fallen into a No-Joke/No-Smile/No-Talk period of his life and the air inside the pickup was tense. When we reached headquarters, Loper was outside, checking his rain gauge.

We unloaded and Slim walked over to him. "How much did you get?"

"Seventy."

"Me too."

"It was a good rain and it'll help."

"I could have spit three times off the porch and it would have been just as good."

Loper poured out the water out of the tube and put it back in its place. "This shortgrass country can do a lot with seventy hundredths."

"Our grass looks pitiful. This is the sorriest country I ever saw. I don't know why anybody ever settled here."

Loper gave him a long glance. "What's eating

on you? You ought to be grateful."

Slim hitched up his jeans. "Well, I ain't. *Bobby Kile got two and a half inches!*"

"How'd you know that?"

"Well, he couldn't wait to drop by the house and ruin my day. He didn't say a word about his rain, so I had to ask. The sneak had it all planned out."

Loper laughed. "You two really have a thing going about rainfall. Didn't he put milk in your rain gauge one time?"

"Yes, and a Cheerio. And right now his pastures probably look like a golf course."

"Covet not thy neighbor's rain."

"Loper, it hurts to miss a rain."

"You didn't miss a rain. You *got* a rain and you're mad about it." Loper wiped his hands on his jeans and glanced around. "So where does that leave us? Should we check you into the hospital for a couple of weeks?"

"I'll get over it. My heart's been broke before. I'm getting used to it."

"Good. Well, here's an idea. How about we shut down the ranch for the day and…go fishing."

Slim gave him a bug-eyed stare. "Fishing! You hate fishing. You ain't got patience enough to bait a hook, much less catch, clean, and cook a fish."

"I have a son who won't stay a little boy for long, and last night he said, 'Daddy, let's go fishing.'"

Slim was biting back a smirk. "Ain't that something! The last time he said that, guess who took him fishing. Me! You went off in New Mexico, looking at bulls. While you were gone, your dog swollered a fish hook and throwed it up on the floorboard of your wife's car, and you'll never guess who got to clean up that mess. Oh yes, we had ourselves a ball. Fishing."

Loper tapped his foot and studied the clouds. "Are you finished?"

"Well, there's more if you want to hear it, but

the main point is that when you start talking about fishing, I ain't thrilled."

Loper nodded and walked a few steps away, stroking his chin. "Alfred's a fine boy."

"He is, and I'm so happy he's got a daddy to take him fishing."

Loper seemed deep in thought. "You get paid by the month, right? And as a loyal employee, you do whatever has to be done on the ranch?"

"Loper, I hired onto this outfit as a *cowboy*. Cowboy. Vaquero. Man a-horseback. Man dressed up in boots and leather and spurs."

"I know, but you have so many talents. And you're right about me. I don't enjoy fishing, but, Slim, I think it would be more enjoyable if I had some adult companionship."

"Loper..."

"With this dry spell and the cattle market down, ranch jobs are kind of scarce, and they say the housing market is pretty tight too." Loper flashed a smile. "Why don't we take Alfred fishing and call it ranch work. We might even have fun."

"I ain't believing this."

"And we're going to camp out."

Slim stared at him. "Why?"

"Because Alfred wants to camp out. He wants to build some childhood memories. I think it's a great idea."

Slim cackled a crazy laugh. "Childhood memories. Do you own any fishing gear or camping stuff?"

"It's been a while since we used it, but I'll bet we can find some. Let's go look."

They marched up the hill to the machine shed, opened the big sliding doors, and went to the northwest corner, where several shelves held piles of ancient stuff that was covered with dust. They plundered through it until they found an old tent, a cast iron skillet, tin plates, a scorched coffee pot, tin cups, and two bamboo fishing poles.

They dragged it outside, into the light, and checked it out. The tent seemed okay, but the fishing gear had gone to ruin, the victim of slow rot, rats, and mice.

Slim seemed pleased. "What did I tell you? People who fish spend money on equipment and spend time keeping it up. You get a wild hair to go fishing once every ten years and this is what happens. You ain't even got a fish hook, so how can you catch a fish?"

Loper gave that some thought. "Surely some of the neighbors have poles and wouldn't mind us borrowing. How about Viola's daddy?"

"Well, he fishes, but don't get any big ideas

about me going down there and mooching his fishing poles."

"How come? He's your future daddy-in-law."

"That's the whole point. Never borrow from your future in-laws. Me and Woodrow get along just fine as long as we're five miles apart and don't borrow."

Loper shrugged. "Okay, I'll ask him. Woodrow and I get along fine."

"'Cause you ain't trying to marry his daughter." They headed back to the house and Slim grumbled, "When does this mess take place?"

"Well, let's get it over with. You load the gear into the pickup and I'll run down to Woodrow's and borrow some poles. We ought to be ready to roll in an hour."

"Had you thought about food?"

"Slim, this isn't church camp. It's an outdoor adventure. We'll eat what we catch."

Slim rolled his eyes. "Loper, let's say that if, by some miracle, you manage to catch a fish. Did you plan to bite off his head and eat him raw? To cook the fish, you'll need grease and cornmeal and salt, and what about coffee? Some of us drink coffee in the morning."

"You make it too complicated."

"Well, by grabs, it is complicated! That's why

we never go fishing. It's too dadgum much trouble. And it's also as boring as watching ants."

"Okay, throw some things together and be ready to leave in an hour. The sooner we get this over with, the better."

Slim shook his head and muttered. "Tonight when you're squirming around on the hard ground, with indigestion, just remember whose big idea this was."

Loper started humming a tune and ignored him. "La la la tee dah."

When we reached the yard gate, Sally May was coming out of the house. She looked pretty solemn and called Loper. He went to the porch and they talked in low voices. She went back into the house and Loper returned to the gate.

"Sally May just got a call from her sister. She's going into labor and we have to drive to Amarillo. I guess the deal's off."

Slim clamped his teeth on a smile. "Well, shucks."

CHAPTER SEVEN

Slim and Woodrow

Well, it appeared that the fishing trip had been cancelled, but just then the back door burst open and here came Little Alfred, his face shining with excitement. He must have heard that I had arrived and was thrilled to see me. You know how it is with kids and dogs. There's a special bond between us and, believe me, I take that part of my job very...

He ran past me and threw his arms around Slim's legs. "Hey Swim, we're going fishing, and we're gonna camp out too!" The boy stepped back and looked up at him, and I mean, the kid's face glowed with joy and excitement. "We're gonna have so much fun!"

Slim's gaze swung around to Loper, who

shrugged. "He doesn't know. You tell him."

Slim knelt down and spoke to the boy. "Hey Button, your folks have to go to Amarillo. Your aunt's fixing to have a baby and your daddy can't go fishing."

"Awwww!" Alfred's eyes darted from one to the other. "Well, I could stay with you."

Loper's eyebrows rose. "I hadn't thought of that."

Slim kept talking. "Button, camping takes a lot of planning and we need a good organizer like your daddy. See, we don't have any fishing gear."

Loper said, "Woodrow."

"And we don't have any bait."

Loper snapped his fingers. "I've heard that canned corn is the best bait in the world, and I'll bet Sally May has some."

"Button, wouldn't you rather wait for a better time?" The boy shook his head. "Well, I've got a feeling your mother wouldn't think too highly of you hanging out with a bachelor."

Loper nodded. "That's a good point. Alfred, go talk to your mom and tell her this will be the adventure of a lifetime. Pour it on. She'll come around." The boy dashed into the house. Loper watched him and nodded. "He's resourceful, he'll get 'er done."

Slim beamed him a cold-eyed glare. "I can't believe you're doing this to me…again."

"Slim, I have no control over women in labor. It's just bad luck." He glanced at his watch. "We need to get on the road. Go talk to Woodrow, gather up your gear, and we'll meet back here in an hour. We'll have Alfred dressed and ready for the experience of a lifetime. Cheer up, Slimbo, you might actually have a good time."

"You're a skunk without stripes."

Loper gave him a wink and a grin. "Be happy in your work."

He went into the house and Slim stomped to his pickup. Naturally, I tagged along behind him. See, I could tell, just by the way he walked, that his mood hadn't gotten any better and might have gotten worse. Drover saw it too and, poof, he vanished like the morning dew, the little weenie.

When Slim jerked open the pickup door, he turned and glared down at me. "Are you follering me around?"

Well…yes, of course. That's what we do. Your higher grades of cowdog are in it for the long haul and we'll be there whether things get bad or worse. And besides, heh heh, I knew there might be a chance that we would get to see Miss Viola.

"Get in."

I flew into the cab and got as far away from him as I could. On the drive down to Woodrow's place, I didn't make a sound and hardly moved a muscle.

"Quit scratching!"

Okay, I scratched ONE TIME and got caught. Sometimes we have to scratch. Is that such a crime? What a grouch.

When we pulled up in front of the house, Miss Viola was working in a flower bed beside the porch. She wore jeans, a pretty red shirt, and a straw hat. When she saw it was me, she flashed a big smile and waved, and naturally I dived out of the pickup and headed toward her in a gallop.

"Hank, leave her alone!"

That was Mister Grumpy McGrumble, of course, and he was jealous that I got a head start. Well, too bad. If he was too lazy to run, that was his problem. She was crazy about me, don't forget, and I hadn't seen her in a week. I knew she'd be...

Huh?

She went past me. Maybe the sun was in her eyes and she didn't see me. Rats. She took Slim's hand and gave him a hug. Rats twice. Hey, what about ME?

She stepped back and looked at him. "What's wrong?"

"Nothing."

"Slim…"

He scuffed up a rock with his boot. "I got rooked into taking the boss's son fishing."

"That's all?"

"That's plenty. Me and fishing don't get along."

"Oh fiddle. You'll have a wonderful time. Is Loper going?"

"Oh sure, he'll be going to Amarillo as fast as the car will run."

"Really? Why?"

"Well, somehow he talked Sally May's sister into having her baby today."

She laughed. "Wait a second. Sally May's sister is having a baby and…how does that fit in with fishing?"

Slim shoved his hands into his pockets and scowled. "I don't know how it fits together, but I know who got stuck with the fishing."

"Slim, I thought all men loved to fish."

"Well, if it was done right, it might be okay, but on our outfit, it's always a slap-dash affair, and it's always a wreck." He told her about the fishing rods. "Mice chewed up the line and pack rats carried off the hooks and bobbers."

"Well, that's a shame. Why don't you borrow ours?"

He rocked up and down on his toes. "Can I borrow from you?"

"Well, it's Daddy's equipment. I'm sure he'd be glad for you to use it."

"I don't want to ask him for favors."

She sighed. "Slim, this is silly but let's don't get into an argument. All right, we'll sneak down to the barn and see if we can find some gear."

"Thanks. Where's Woodrow?"

"The last I saw, he was inside, drinking coffee and reading *Livestock Weekly*."

"Good." He patted her on the shoulder. "You're a pal."

She raised one eyebrow and gave him That Look. "I'd better be more than a pal, mister."

"Okay, you're a good pal."

She gave him a swat on the arm and they walked down to the barn. Nobody said I couldn't go, so I went. They opened the door and stepped inside and…oops, who should be sitting at the work bench but Woodrow. He was sorting a bunch of rusted bolts, nuts, and washers and putting them into coffee cans.

Slim stopped dead in his tracks and his eyeballs almost fell out on the floor. Woodrow looked at him through shaggy eyebrows. "Huh. What are you doing here? You lost?"

"Why, good morning, Woodrow." He swallowed hard and shot a glance at Viola. "No, I was just wondering…I was thinking of going fishing and wondered if I could borrow a few things."

"I thought you had a job."

"Well, I do and this is part of it."

"Huh. I never had that kind of job. Must be nice."

"The boss wants me to take his boy fishing, see."

"How come he don't do it himself?"

Viola's eyebrow flew up again. "Daddy! He wants to borrow some tackle."

The old man sat back in his chair. "What do you need?"

"Two poles rigged up."

"So you need everything?"

"That's about the size of it."

"I ain't got poles. I've got rods and reels, good ones. They cost a chunk of money. What kind of fish are you going after?"

"The kind a boy can catch in the creek."

"Catfish? Perch? Bass? It makes a difference."

"Perch."

Woodrow pushed himself out of the chair and ambled over to a closet. He brought out two shiny rods and reels. "How come you don't have any fishing gear?"

"Well, the mice got into it."

Woodrow shot him a hard glare. "Tell your mice to stay out of my stuff and bring it back clean. And soon."

"Yes sir."

Slim couldn't wait to get out of there. Hee hee. It was funny. Boy, he was sweating. As he was going out the door, Woodrow growled, "How much rain did you get?"

"Seventy hundredths."

The old man barked a laugh. "I got an inch and a half. The Lord knows who to bless."

"Thanks, Woodrow."

CHAPTER EIGHT

Major Preparations

Poor Slim! His day had started badly and it seemed to be getting worse. Outside, he and Viola headed for the pickup and she said, "I had no idea he was in the barn. I'm sorry."

"That's okay. We got the frazzling poles."

"I thought he was rude, asking all those questions."

"He was just being Woodrow."

"Well, he's fussy about his equipment. He's always been that way, even with his own daughters."

Slim gave her a hard look. "Did y'all actually get an inch and a half of rain, or was he just loadin' me?"

"I think we did. It was a nice rain."

"Everybody in Texas got a nice rain, except us."

"Are you going to let that spoil your day?"

"I might, but there's always the chance this fishing deal will make it worse. We'll have to see."

She laughed. "It's too bad you can't see yourself. This is so funny!"

"Good."

We had reached the pickup by then and...get this...Viola knelt down and opened her arms to... well, to ME! "Bye, Hank, give me a hug."

Wow, did you hear that? At last she'd noticed me! I flew into her awaiting arms and she hugged my neck and I licked her ears and it was just the way I'd always imagined it could be. Didn't I tell you she was crazy about me?

She fluffed my ears. "You're such a sweet dog, but you have to live with a grouchy old bachelor."

Exactly right! Maybe we could ditch Slim and move to a castle on a mountaintop and live happily everly after.

She stood up and brushed some dog hair off her hands and turned a smile on Mister Grump. "Cheer up, Slim, and enjoy the things you have. You'll get a big rain one of these days and you can call Daddy and ruin his day." She stood on tip-toes and gave him a kiss on the cheek.

"That wasn't much of a kiss."

"Well, that's all you get. Work on your attitude

and give your dog a bath sometime. Bye bye."

She fluttered her fingers at him and went back to the flowerbed.

We loaded into the pickup and headed up the creek. As we pulled away from the house, Slum grimbled...Slim grumbled, "I can't believe that old goat got an inch and a half! And he loved telling me. I should have made him go first. Never go first on rainfall, pooch. The first liar don't have a chance."

Okay, I would try to remember that. Actually, I had no idea what he was talking about. That happens a lot around here.

Then he added, "You need to take a bath sometime. The ladies ain't impressed by dogs who stink."

Oh brother.

We made a stop at Slim's place and he threw together some supplies for the big camping expedition: flour, salt, and grease, a kerosene lantern, matches, a sleeping bag, and a pillow. Then he went into the kitchen and found a bottle of ketchup. "Veshtables for the boy." He looked in a cabinet and came out with a can of mackerel. "Just in case the fishies don't show up, we'll have a backup."

Gag. Have we discussed canned mackerel? I mean, it smells worse than cat food but he keeps twelve cans of it in the cabinet...and eats it! Why? Because it's cheap, and why wouldn't it be cheap? It's nothing but dead fish in a can.

But it's also easy to fix: open the can, shovel the dead fish onto a slice moldy bread, slop on some mustard or ketchup, and maybe a pickle if he's feeling gourmet, and pile on another slice of bread. At that point, he opens his mouth like a shark and takes a chomp. Three more chomps and dinner is history.

It's Bachelor Dream Food: cheap, easy, and no dishes to wash. He can sweep the crumbs onto the floor and give the mackerel juice to the dogs. Like dummies, we lap it up and get indigestion.

Yes, I admit that I've been lured into this on a few occasions and always regretted it. If he planned to serve canned mackerel for supper tonight, he didn't need to worry about me stealing his camp meat. I had been to school on mackerel.

That done, we left the house and Slim spent ten minutes looking for his rain gauge, the one he'd thrown away in a childish fit of temper. He finally located it in the horse lot and it wasn't broken. He put it back in its holder and growled, "Not that we'll ever need it again."

Then we drove back to ranch headquarters. Little Alfred was waiting for us in the yard, pacing around and watching for our pickup. I mean, the kid was wired up for the fishing trip.

Loper was coming out of the house with luggage and not looking happy. That brought a smirk to Slim's face, the nearest thing to a smile we'd seen all day. By the time Loper got to the car, Slim was slouched against the back door. "Did you remember to pack the kitchen sink?"

"Make yourself useful and open the door."

"Please?"

"Open the door."

Slim opened the door and Loper pitched the bags inside. Slim watched and slid a toothpick around in his mouth. "I've read that when Cleopatra went for a morning ride on her barge, it took ten head of servants to load her stuff."

"Your time's coming, cowboy, and I hope I'm around to enjoy the paybacks."

"How many weeks do y'all planned to stay gone?"

"Hush. Did you get the fishing stuff from Woodrow?"

"Ten-four. And I stopped at my place and got a bunch of other things you never would have thought of."

"Ten bucks says you didn't pack any *soap*." Long silence. Loper barked a laugh. "Just what

I figured. You owe me ten bucks." He glanced at his watch. "That baby'll be in kindergarten before we get there."

"Woodrow got an inch and a half of rain."

"Good. That'll give you something else to

whine about. Maybe you'll get a big rain tonight, while you're camped out."

Slim looked up at the sky. "Not a chance. The wind's out of the southwest and them's drought clouds. There wouldn't be a raindrop in a whole trainload of 'em."

At last, Sally May came out of the house, carrying her purse and Baby Molly and the diaper bag. She came out the gate and handed everything to Loper. "I need to water the flowers. It won't take but a minute."

Loper's eyes bulged. "Hon, we got rain last night and we need to get on the road."

"They look dry."

"Slim can water the tulips. Let's load and go. Slim, water the tulips."

Slim rolled his eyes.

Sally May knelt down and pulled Alfred into a hug. "Sweetie, we'll miss you very much, but I know you'll have a wonderful time," she shot a glance at Slim, "camping out. Don't go into deep water and brush your teeth."

"Okay, Mom. We'll be fine."

She stood up and faced Slim. "I'm sure he'll get something to eat."

"Oh yes ma'am. We're going to catch a bunch of fish, and I even brought some veshtables."

"Slim, I must be honest…"

Loper's voice cracked. "Sally May, your sister's fixing to have a baby, let's go."

She gave Alfred another kiss and stepped into the car. Loper tossed one last glance at Slim and said, "Happy fishing, and try not to do anything stupid while I'm gone." And off they went to the big city of Amarillo.

Alfred watched as the car roared away. "Hey Swim, what's scurvy?"

"Where'd you hear that word?"

"My mom's afraid I'm going to catch it."

Slim grunted a laugh. "No kidding? It's a little bug that bites and sucks your blood. They love naughty-little-boy blood, so you'd better behave yourself."

The boy looked up at him. "Aw. Are you fooling me?"

"Honest. I saw three scurvies this morning, and they might have been looking for you."

Alfred studied him closer and saw a little slice of a grin. "You're teasing me."

"Yalp, you caught me." He hitched up his jeans. "I think your ma don't trust my cooking and thinks you'll come down with some dreaded jungle disease."

"Really? Will I?"

"Not a chance. Me and you are going to catch so many fish, we won't need to eat again for two months."

"You're gonna cook 'em?"

"Unless you want to eat 'em raw. Some people just swaller 'em alive and let 'em swim around in their stomach."

The boy shook his head. "Nuh uh. You're teasing again."

"Well, of course we're going to cook 'em. We'll fry 'em up in hot grease till they're crisp and juicy, but we have to catch 'em first. Don't forget that part."

Alfred raised his eyebrows and lowered his voice. "I know a secret."

"Oh you do, do you?"

"Yep. There's a quart of ice cream in the freezer and I'm hungry."

Slim gave that some thought. "Are you wanting to get us scalped?"

"Maybe my mom won't notice."

Slim laughed. "Button, your ma knows everything about everything that happens in her house and yard."

"She forgets sometimes."

There was a long moment of silence. "What religion of ice cream are we talking about?"

Alfred grinned. "Peach."

"Uh oh. Well, that's going to put me in a real bind, 'cause I like peach ice cream about as much as anything I know. And nobody served breakfast at my camp this morning."

The boy took hold of Slim's finger and started tugging him toward the house. "Come on, Swim."

CHAPTER NINE

Peach Ice Cream!

S lim resisted for about two seconds, then followed. "Well, it says in the Bible 'the little children will lead them,' so I guess it's okay. But we ain't going to eat ice cream in your ma's house. If she was to find one drip on her floor, she'd smell a rat."

"Okay, Swim."

"I don't care if you get scalped, but if I lost all my hair, my hat wouldn't fit."

"Really?"

"Oh yeah, and I'd have to drive all the way into town to shop for a new one, and I hate to shop."

"Then we'll eat on the porch."

They went into the house and I began licking my chops. Wow, this was going to be the best camping trip in history. Peach ice cream on the porch for breakfast!

They had left the yard gate open and Sally May had left the ranch, so I oozed myself through the gate, into the yard, and set up a scout position near the door. I figured that with a little boy and a bachelor cowboy involved in this deal, my odds of getting into the ice cream were pretty good.

And don't forget that I was starved, hadn't eaten in days and weeks, no kidding.

I was sitting there, waiting for my guys to come out with the loot, when I heard a voice to my left. "Well, well, it's Hankie the Wonderdog!"

I whipped my head around and saw…can you guess? Mister Never Sweat. Mister Kitty Moocher. Sally May's rotten little cat. He was occupying his favorite loafing spot on the ranch, the iris patch, and here he came, rubbing his way down the side of the house and purring like a little chainsaw. And smirking, always smirking.

The sight of him set off lip seizures on my mouthalary region, lips that were aching to rise and reveal two rows of intercontinental ballistic fangs. That's the effect he has on me.

Have we discussed my Position On Cats? I don't like 'em, never have.

Naturally he began running his mouth right away. "Hankie, you're in Sally May's yard, and she doesn't allow dogs in the yard."

"That's correct, Kitty, but she's not here. In her absence, I'll be taking over all yard business and responsibilities."

"Oh really. I doubt that she'd approve."

"I doubt that she'll know, which is bad news for the local cats. Things are going to be different around here."

"My, my. Anything I should know about?"

"I'm glad you asked. Number One, wipe that smirk off your mouth."

"Me? Was I smirking?"

"Wipe it off, and don't forget there's a tree on the north side of the house."

"And you might run me up the tree?"

"Roger that. Get rid of the smirk." He wiped a paw over his mouth and the smirk disappeared. "Good, we're making progress. Number Two, sit down, stand up straight, and salute your superior officer."

"Hankie, if I sit down, how can I stand up straight?"

"You figure it out." He sat down, stood up straight, and made a pretty good salute. "Wait. Did you cross your eyes?"

"I think maybe I did, Hankie."

I moved closer and glared right into his

cheating little face. "Don't cross your eyes when you're saluting a superior officer."

"But this is painful, Hankie."

"Nobody cares. Salute." He did his salute and didn't cross his eyes. "That's better. Number Three, you get no peach ice cream."

He glanced around. "Are we having peach ice cream?"

"Some of us are. My men are rounding up ice cream as we speak and will be here shortly. You get none, zero ice cream. We're going to eat in front of you and you're going to be miserable."

Hee hee. Boy, this was fun. When Sally May and her broom are out of the picture, I can get a lot accomplished around here.

Just then, my guys came out of the house, wearing huge grins and holding big spoons and, mercy, the boy was carrying a whole quart of ice cream. They flopped down on the porch steps and Alfred pried off the lid.

His eyes were dancing and he held the spoon in his fist. "Welp, here goes!" He dug in and came up with a big hunk, shoved it into his mouth and said, "Oh, wat wood!"

"Say what?"

He chewed it up. "I said, oh, that's good. You better get some, Swim."

"Okay, here comes my backhoe."

Slim dug and ate. The boy dug and ate. I watched, whapped my tail, moved my front paws up and down, and tried my very best to do Patient Doggie, but it was tough.

At last Alfred noticed me. "Hankie, you want a bite?"

Oh, well, maybe, if it wasn't too much...YES!

"Swim, should I give Hankie a bite?"

"Well, it's your spoon and I guess you can do whatever you want with it. He ain't eating out of mine. But let me point out that your momma wouldn't approve."

"Oh, I don't think she'd mind. She likes Hankie."

Slim made a kind of snorting sound and took another bite. "Well, you'd better do it then."

Alfred shoveled out a big glob of pink material that sent a blast of sweet fumes into the noselary tunnels of my nose. "Okay, Hankie, try this."

Snarf! I snagged it, spoon and all, and you talk about something that was sweetly and peachly delicious, this was it!

"Give my spoon back!"

Fine, take the spoon. Dogs don't eat spoons. Great stuff!

Then the boy noticed his mother's pampered, rotten little cat sitting nearby. "Hey Pete, you

want some ice cream?"

I could hardly control myself, I mean, the ice cream had been great, but this was the Really Good Part of the show. When Kitty took a bite—against my strict orders—I would have no choice but to intervene and run him up the nearest tree, and this would produce a major Tee-Hee Situation.

The boy dug out some ice cream and moved the spoon toward the cat. The muscles in my enormous body grew tense and I prepared to launch the weapon. The greedy little...

Huh?

Get this. The cat turned up his nose and walked away! Then he smirked at me and said—this is a direct quote—he said, "I don't eat ice cream, Hankie. It gives me a headache."

I was speechless. My mind tumbled and for a second, I had a strong irremuckable feeling that, well, somehow he had slithered past my trap, so I said the first thing that came to mind. "Let that be a lesson, you little reptile!"

Dumb cat.

Oh well, that left more ice cream for me and my guys, and we got after it. Alfred and I found a nice rhythm: one for him, one for me, back and forth. And Slim was holding up his end of the deal, really scooping it in. See, he was too cheap to buy his own ice cream, so when he had a chance to dip into Sally May's inventory, he kind of lost his mind.

Between scoops, he said, "Boy, this is some kind of fine cowboy breakfast. I'll bet them big ranches down south don't feed this good." He licked the spoon and raised it in the air. "You know, Button, this is so much fun, maybe we ought to forget the fishing trip."

Alfred stared at him and shook his head. "Uh uh. My dad said we're going fishing."

"I know, but it's liable to get pretty hot…and we don't have any bait."

"My dad found a can of corn."

"The scrounge." He peeked into the container. "Say, somebody put a big dent in that ice cream. Reckon we ought to finish it off?"

The boy nodded. "Yeah, then we can throw away the carton and maybe my mom won't notice."

"I think that's a good plan, but if she happens to notice, I want the record to show that I was against it."

We got back to work, one bite for me, one for Alfred, one for…ouch. You know, it was the craziest thing, but all at once I had this…this headache, you might say. And a tiny voice in my mind whispered, "If you eat too much ice cream, too fast, it'll give you a headache."

It was no big deal, I mean, it happens in the best of families. If you eat too much ice cream, too fast, it'll give you a headache. It has something to do with…I don't know what it has something to do with, but it happens all the time and everybody knows about it.

It's not a big deal. I've already said that, but important concepts should be emphasized. Furthermore, I'm Head of Ranch Security and if I want to repeat myself repeat myself, I will I will. So there. The impointant pork is that getting an Ice Cream Headache is no big deal.

I happened to glance around and noticed…the cat. He wore an even smirkier smirk than before, and fluttered his eyelashes. "Is something wrong, Hankie?"

Was that enough of a provocation to cause the Security Division to scramble jets and park the little sneak in a tree? I mean, we knew he knew about the Ice Cream Headache and was trying make a big deal out of it, even though we had already worked through it and proved it was NBD (No Big Deal, in case you're not familiar with our terminology).

My eyes darted back and forth, and the entire unit waited to see if gongs would start gonging.

I'm sure you're aching to find out if we Launched All Dogs, so you'd better keep reading.

CHAPTER TEN

Drover Is Mathematically Impossible

No. The gongs didn't gong. We got the order to Stand Down and ignore the cat. Finishing our mission on the ice cream was just too important to allow us to be distracted by the little pestilence.

I waved and smiled. "Doing fine, Kitty, but thanks for your concern. We're thinking about you on every bite."

Hee hee! Oh, I blew him away with that one, mopped the floor with him, left him hissing and speechless! Hee hee! I'm sure it ruined his day and maybe his whole...

Huh?

Good grief, unless I was badly mistaken, Little Alfred was scraping his spoon around the bottom of an empty carton. In other words, whilst I'd been distracted by the cat, my two so-called friends had hogged it all.

Okay, maybe I'd done my share of the damage, but don't forget the Wise Old Saying: "The hogger the hog, the dogger the dog." Hmm. That doesn't make sense, does it? It rhymes and it's got a cute little bounce, but it doesn't make sense, so let's skip it. Forget the WOS.

The point is that when you've got one cowboy, one little boy, and one ranch dog working on a quart of ice cream, the ice cream has no chance. It will lose every time. Gone. Poof. With great sadness, I watched as the boy spooned out the last of the cream on the bottom and licked the spoon with his…well, with his tongue, of course. What else would you…never mind.

Who or whom do you suppose showed up at that very moment? Drover. Where had he been for the past thirty minutes? We never know. His tongue was hanging out one side of his mouth and his eyes blazed with a greedy light. "Oh goodie, ice cream! Boy, I love ice cream."

"Well, that's too bad, because this ice cream won't be loving you back."

His face collapsed like the roof of a sand cave. "You mean…"

"I mean it's gone, poof, empty."

"Y'all ate the whole thing?"

"That is bork correct, excuse me, and it was some great stuff. Peach."

He fell over and started kicking all four legs. "Oh darn, no fair! I never get to eat peach ice cream."

"When you wander away from your unit, you miss out on the action. You have no one to blame but your borp. Yourself."

"And now you're burping in front of me, just to rub it in!"

"Drover, those were sounds of satisfaction and they popped out by accident. They weren't meant to cause you any pain."

He sat up and swiped a paw over his tear-streaked face. "Well, maybe I'll get over it."

"I know you will, because you have no choice. We live in the Real World and it's really worldly."

"What does that mean?"

"The Real World is the realest thing we know about."

"What about ice cream?"

"Ice cream is one of the realest things in the Real World, but when it's gone, we have to let it go."

He still looked sad. "Yeah, but you burped in front of me, twice."

"All right, I'm sorry I burped in front of you twice."

"Honest? You're not just saying that?"

I paced a few steps away and struggled with this. "Okay, the truth is that I enjoyed burping in front of you, because I enjoyed the ice cream. This is America, Drover, where dogs are still free to burp in public about their ice cream experiences, and you need to grow up and join the Real World, because there's no place else to go."

"What about the machine shed?"

"You have your Secret Sanctuary in the machine shed, but it's not part of the Real World."

"It has a real chair. That's where I hide."

"Drover, listen to me. You're trying to use a real chair to hide from the Real World and that is mathematically impossible."

"Yeah, but I do it all the time, hee hee."

"Exactly my point. You have made yourself mathematically impossible. No wonder you've turned out to be such a goofball. You're living in defiance of the Laws of Figgy."

"What's Figgy?"

I glared at him for a long moment. "After all these years in Security Work, and you're still asking what is Figgy?"

"Yeah, I never heard of it. Maybe you meant physics."

I stormed over to him and screamed in his face. "Are you listening to this conversation? We're babbling like lunatics and I have NO IDEA what we're talking about!"

"Well, you burped and said I was mathematically impossible. It really hurt my feelings."

I tried to put a leash on my temper, walked a few steps away, and took in a deep calming breath of carbon diego. My whole body was shaking. "All right, we've got to work our way out of this. Here's a plan. We'll both be sorry that I burped in front of you and we'll both disregard what I said about you being mathematically impossible. Would that make you feel better?"

"Well, let me check." He rolled his eyes around. "Oh yeah, I'm already feeling more like I do right now than I did a while ago."

"Good, good. That's a positive sign." I paced back to him and laid a paw on his shoulder. "Drover, we've got to stop having these conversations. If someone heard us, they might get the wrong impression."

"Yeah, they might think we're a couple of dumb dogs."

"Exactly, and that could have a terrible effect on the morale of this unit, so let's keep it to ourselves, behind closed doors."

"Yeah, but we don't have any doors."

"I understand, but it's important that we have goals to strive for. Our goal for the week will be… doors."

"Doors?"

"That's correct."

"Where do dogs get doors?"

"Drover, no more, not another word. Let's put this behind us and go out there and make the world a better place."

"The Real World?"

"Yes, let's start there and we'll branch out later."

I whirled around and marched away. The little mutt was a certified lunatic.

CHAPTER ELEVEN

Kitty Gets Drenched Hee Hee!

My mind had become a bowl of scrambled eggs. Did any of that make sense to you? Not to me. Viewed from a certain angle, it sounded...well, crazy. What else could you call it? I don't know how he draws me into these bozo conversations, but he does it all the time and I'll be honest, it worries me.

Now, where were we in this story? I have no idea. None. It's as though someone had emptied my head and filled it with water and goldfish.

Wait. The fishing trip. Drover had led me into a dangerous dog-fog and but now we'd emerged back into the light of day, and I mean a normal day, the kind that happens when he's not around.

Maybe you had forgotten, but the entire ranch

was getting ready for a fishing and camping expedition and that was big news. It doesn't happen around here very often, because our cowboy crew doesn't know how to play or have fun, and that's one of the big reasons that every ranch needs dogs and little boys—to lead iron-headed cowboys out of their Ruts of Life and introduce them to joyful experiences.

So let's get on with the joyful experiences.

After surviving that loony conversation with Drover, I joined Slim and Little Alfred. If you remember, Loper had told Slim to water Sally May's turnips...tulips...whatever she had growing in her flowerbeds. That's what Slim was doing when I arrived, spraying the flowers with the hose.

Alfred watched, yawned, glanced around, and dug his hands into the pockets of his striped overalls. "Hey Swim, hurry up. This is boring."

"Your ma wanted her posies watered and that's what I'm a-doing. You probably don't want to go fishing anyway."

"Oh yes I do, and you promised." The boy's gaze drifted to the iris patch. His eyes popped open and a wicked little grin sliced across his mouth.

You might not believe this, but I knew what the little snipe was thinking, I mean, dogs *know*.

He said, "Hey Swim, let me spray for a while."

"Fine with me, spray all you want."

The lad took the hose and adjusted the spray nozzle from fine mist to fire hose. Have you figured it out? Hee hee! What a fine young man! He jacked up the force of the water, don't you see, sprayed his way down the side of the house, and FIRE-HOSED his momma's rotten little cat, I mean blasted him! Kitty never saw it coming. Do you know why?

1. Cats are DUMB, and we're talking about dumber-than-dirt dumb.
2. Cats don't understand little boys. I mean, when you give a boy a water hose and there's a cat around, what do you think will happen? Duh.
3. Cats are so consumed with their own plots and schemes, it never occurs to them that anyone else in the world might be plotting and scheming.
4. And finally, cats are dumb. We've already listed that, but it it's important enough to mention again.

Anyway, Kitty got blasted and went off like a coiled spring, jumped three feet straight up in the air, hissing and yowling. Even at a distance, I could see that his coat of hair had melted into a soggy mess and his whiskers were pasted against his cheating little face. What a delicious sight! I loved it.

I decided to rub it in. "There you go, Kitty, a little valentine from the Security Division! If there's anything else we can do to ruin your day, just let us know. Hee hee!"

Did I get him told or what? I got him told.

In mid-air, Kitty beamed me a murderous glare, so I returned fire—stuck out my tongue and crossed my eyes, bang bang, one right after the other. It was devastating. He crashed back into the iris patch and high-balled it around the north side of the house in total defeat. It was one of the most...

SPLAT!

Okay, the kid was having such a big time, he swung the hose around and blasted ME. On the one hand, I must admit that, well, it caught us by surprise and I got creamed. But on the other hand, it made perfect sense. He was a ranch kid. That's what they do and we dogs understand their ways because, in the same situation, we would do the same thing.

By the way, Drover, the King of Weenies, got off without a drop of water. He saw it coming and slunk away. Slinked. Slank. I don't know how he does it, but it happens all the time.

Slank.

Slim shut off the water and wiped his hands on his jeans. "Well, Button, how's about we grab a nice long nap and spend the afternoon checking windmills?" The boy set his jaw and shook his head. "You're sure about that?" The boy gave his head an emphatic nod. "What did you have in mind?"

"Fishing, and you know it."

Slim heaved a sigh and jingled some coins in his pocket. "What if we was to drive into town and get a big old greasy hamburger?"

"Swim!"

"Fishing. Okay, let's get it over with, but we ain't taking those dogs. All they know about camping is to bark all night and eat fish hooks. Remember that fish hook deal?"

Alfred said nothing but put his arm around my neck, held me tight, and pressed his cheek against my face. It was one of the sweetest, tenderest scenes you could ever imagine. A boy and his dog!

Slim groaned. "Oh, spare me. Fine, take your stinking dogs, but they ain't sleeping in my tent."

"Thanks, Swim. You're a nice man."

He stomped out the yard gate and we followed. He was on a snort. "Yes, and I want it wrote on my tombstone, 'Old Slim wasn't smart or rich, he died broke and never amounted to much, but he was always nice to bratty little boys and soup hounds.' You make sure they get it right. Oh, and add one more thing. 'He always wanted to be a cowboy but they turned him into a babysitter and a fishing guide.' I want future generations to know the kind of suffering I had to endure."

Alfred and I traded glances and he laughed. "He gets silly."

Yes, he certainly did.

We went up to the machine shed and Slim chunked a few more items into the back of the pickup: a ballpeen hammer for driving tent stakes, a shovel for trenching the tent, and a slab of plywood for cleaning fish.

Drover showed up about then, from where we didn't know, and wondered what was going on. I told him and he wrinkled up his nose. "Not me. I'm scared of fish, and they stink."

"Too bad. Little Alfred wants his dogs along and you *will* attend."

"Oh drat."

"Drover, I've warned you about cursing and swearing on the job. Five Chicken Marks."

"Oh poodle."

"Ten Chicken Marks."

"What's wrong with saying 'poodle'?"

"We don't like poodles. Is that what you want to be when you grow up?"

"Well…"

"Load into the pickup, soldier, and no more whining."

Oh brother. You see what I have to put up with?

The three of us loaded into the back of the pickup and off we went on this great new adventure, fishing and camping with our little pal…and with a grumpy cowboy who still hadn't recovered from his Morning Tragedy, getting beaten on rainfall by two of the neighbors. That had been the start of his slide into gloom and it had lasted all day.

Now, he was riding by himself in the cab, gripping the steering wheel with both hands, glaring out at the pasture, and mumbling words we couldn't hear.

Wait. Was he singing? Yes, he was sitting alone in the cab and singing. Listen.

Wishin' I Wasn't Goin' Fishin'

I'm wishin' I wasn't going fishin'.
I'm wishin' I was home instead
Sittin' out on the porch in my underwear
Or curled up and snoozing in my bed.

It's not that I'm against having fun.
I don't enjoy getting broiled in the sun
Or getting ate alive by a bunch of
    hungry flies
Or taking little bitty perch off the hook.

I'm thinkin' that soon I'll be stinkin'
Of fish guts and musketeer dope.
I'll probably have to take another bath
  tomorrow
And waste another half bar of soap.

A cowboy ought to be in the saddle,
Prowling pastures and checking the
    cattle.
Babysitting's for the birds and it's
    totally absurd
To waste the time of a man of my talent.

I'm wishin' I hadn't listened
To the boss when he told me to take
His bratty little son on a fishing trip,
Should have told him to go jump in the lake.

Should have told him to go jump in the lake.
But then I might be unemployed.

Well, it wasn't a great musical experience but not the worst song he'd ever come up with, I mean the guy was the King of The Corny Song. Actually, I thought it was pretty funny.

Anyway, we headed toward what was probably the best fishing hole on the ranch, a place south of the house where the creek formed a nice pool. Even in a dry spell, it remained pretty wide and pretty deep, and you might remember that we had fished there before.

That was the place where I swallowed...that is, where I was infected with the Fish Hook Virus, shall we say. Bad deal and it required emergency medical services: Slim forced me to swallow a bunch of liquid soap, but that's another story.

When we got there, Alfred was so excited, he could hardly stand still while Slim rigged up the fishing gear. Slim hadn't remembered to bring a can opener, so he had to open the can of bait (corn) by hacking off the lid with his pocket knife and a pair of fencing pliers. Then he baited the hook with a piece of corn and gave the boy some instructions on how to use a rod and reel.

"It belongs to my future daddy-in-law, so keep it clean and don't get the line tangled up. If a big alligator comes along and wants to eat you, try to save the rod and reel."

"Swim, we don't have alligators."

"Well, you never know. If you're scared, we can go check windmills."

The boy studied him long enough to decide that he was joking, grabbed the pole, let out a yell, and dashed to the creek. You'll never guess what happened next. Keep reading.

The Camp
Gets Lost

A re you ready for this?

What happened next was that Alfred made his cast into the pool and started *catching fish*! It was amazing. All at once, everything was working just the way it's supposed to work on a fishing trip: we had good equipment, the fish were biting corn, and I was there to bark every fish out of the water. (Drover sat off to himself, staring at the clouds and snapping at flies).

Alfred was having a blast and even Slim got into the spirit of things. Hey, he started smiling! Yes, I saw it with my own eyes. After all the moaning and bellyaching he'd done, after all the "poor me" and "I hate fishing," he was actually enjoying himself.

Alfred did all the catching and Slim took care of the other chores: took the fish off the hook, reloaded the bait, and either tossed the small fish back into the creek or put the big ones on a stringer. He was so busy, he never got around to rigging up his own line.

At first we were catching little bluegill perch, most too small to eat but some of them big enough to keep. Then the bass started hitting the corn and the boy pulled out some nice ones—not huge, but just the right size to fit a skillet. Along toward evening, Slim pulled the stringer of fish out of the creek and held it up for Alfred to see.

"Lookie here, Button, you've caught our dinner. We won't have to eat canned mackerel."

The boy stared at all those fish, held his head up proud, flashed a big grin, and thumped himself on the chest. The Mighty Fisherman! I was proud too, I mean, that was My Kid who'd caught all those fish. Drover was chasing a grasshopper and missed the whole show. He's such a...never mind.

Slim let down the tail gate on the pickup and used it as his table for cleaning fish. And fellers, the work began. In case you didn't know, fish that come fresh out of the creek aren't ready to eat. Somebody has to remove the guts and heads, cut off the fins, and scrape off the scales with a knife. And it gets messy.

Slim cleaned the first ten and showed Alfred how to do it, then the boy took over and cleaned a bunch by himself. When the job was done, we had a nice pile of twenty fish that were ready for frying, and Alfred was a happy little boy...and filthy. By then, he had more fish scales than the fish did. He had to strip down to his shorts and take a bath in the creek.

Slim gathered up wood and started a campfire, and the air turned soft and sweet with the smell of smoke from cedar and cottonwood limbs. Oh, by the way, one of the first things that went into the fire was the empty ice cream carton. Slim and Alfred had planned it all out, don't you see: destroy the evidence and maybe Sally May wouldn't notice.

My answer to that was...ha! They didn't know her as well as I did.

When the fire died down to coals, Slim made a hearth of rocks and set the big cast iron skillet over the coals. He powdered up the fish with cornmeal and salt, and when the grease was popping, he laid the fish into the grease, and my oh my, the smells got better and better.

He brought them out of the skillet, golden brown, and placed them into a couple of tin plates. He showed the boy how to scrape the meat off one side, then lift out the backbone and ribs, and they got down to some serious eating.

I watched this with, uh, considerable interest, shall we say, and after they had eaten five or six fish apiece, they started sharing. They pitched chunks of meat to me and Drover, and I had to admit that old Slim had a talent for frying fish.

By the way, I snagged my bites out of the air and Drover's bounced off his nose. He has never figured out how to catch food out of the air.

When we'd eaten all we could eat, they sand-washed the plates and wiped out the skillet with a grease rag, then went to work setting up the tent. By the time the shadows started growing long, we had ourselves a genuine fishing camp on the banks of Wolf Creek.

Slim lit the kerosene lantern and chunked up the fire, and we watched the stars come out. Drover chased bugs and sparks from the fire, and Slim told some ghost stories. I could see the fire light dancing in Alfred's eyes. "See, Swim, isn't this fun?"

Slim poked at the fire with a stick. "Well, I don't want anyone to quote me on this, but it's turned out to be a pretty fine day. Fishing ain't as bad as I remembered. I think even your daddy

might have enjoyed it."

The boy yawned. "Do you think it's going to rain?"

Slim laughed. "Not a chance. It ain't ever going to rain again. Let's turn in."

Great idea! Slim had called it a "pup" tent, so I figured it was designed mostly for dogs. I was the first camper inside the tent and was scratching up a spot on the sleeping bag....

"Hank, outside, scram!"

...but decided to give up my bed for the guys. It was kind of a small tent, don't you see, and you know me. I ride for the brand.

The lights went out, the guys moved into the tent, the stars twinkled, and the crickets chirped. It was a perfect happy ending to one of the best camp-outs ever held on my ranch, and that's about all of the story.

Well, almost. Around five o'clock in the morning, a canon went off, the sky lit up, Drover let out a screech, and it started raining. Pretty hard. Within minutes, we were wet and what's a dog supposed to do? Well, we slithered our way inside the tent, is what we did, and don't forget that it was a *pup* tent, designed for dogs.

In a flash of lightning, I saw Slim sit straight up in bed. "Good honk, is that rain? Hey, Button, we're getting a little shower."

The boy blinked his eyes and yawned. "I thought you said it wasn't going to rain."

"Well, I missed my forecast and all I can say is halleluiah! Now we can go back to sleep and listen to the sound of rain. Those dogs stink, but I don't care. Let 'er rain!"

So we settled in and went back to sleep,

listening to the clatter of rain on the tent. Actually, it became more of a steady roar than a clatter, and I began to suspect that it was turning into more than a "little shower."

It must have been, oh, an hour later when I heard Alfred's voice. "Hey Swim, it's wet in here."

"Tent leaks. Go back to sleep."

Several minutes passed. The rain roared, lighting popped, the wind screamed, and thunder crashed, and I heard the boy's voice again. "Hey Swim, I think the creek's coming into the tent."

That woke him up. He sat straight up, fumbled around for his flashlight, and switched it on. All four of us stared at...well, it appeared that Wolf Creek was running through the middle of our tent.

"Good Granny Grayback, the creek's rising! We need to get out of here! Run for the pickup, kid!"

Maybe they shouldn't have pitched the tent on a sandbar right next to the creek, but Slim *knew* it was never going to rain again, so what could go wrong? Duh. If he had asked his dogs for advice, I would have told him...but it was too late for that. The creek was flooding and the horse was already out of the toothpaste.

Slim grabbed his boots and clothes and took Alfred's hand and we sloshed our way through foot-deep water and past chunks of driftwood. When we reached the pickup, the water was already up to the hubcaps. Slim struggled with the door and got it open, and we all climbed inside, drenched and dripping and cold.

He turned the ignition key and the motor growled. Rurr, rurr, rurr. It didn't start! Good grief, we were going to get washed away in the terrible…

But then the motor started. Whew! Slim turned on the headlights and windshield wipers, threw the transfer case lever into four-wheel drive, and we plowed our way to higher ground. It was a good thing he knew the pasture and the lay of the land, because he couldn't see much of anything in the headlights, I mean, it was raining snakes and weasels and pitchforks.

We crept along through the pasture and finally made it back to headquarters and parked in front of the machine shed. Slim left the motor running and turned on the heater and let out a big breath of air.

"Well, I wanted a rain and I got it. Teach me to complain. I guess we can kiss that tent goodbye. It'll take out every watergap between here and Ft. Smith, Arkansas." His eyes popped open. "Good honk, Woodrow's fishing rods!" He slapped his forehead with the palm of his hand.

Oops.

Well, we spent what was left of the night in the pickup. Come morning, sunlight sparkled on fresh green grass in the pastures, the creek was spread out like a river, and our tent was on its way to Ft. Smith, along with a bunch of camping gear and Woodrow's fishing rods.

Loper and Sally May made it home in the afternoon and had to plow their way through five miles of muddy road. The rain and green grass put Loper in high spirits and he laughed his head off when Slim and Alfred told about our camp getting washed away in the flood.

He stopped laughing when Slim told him that he was going to have to buy Woodrow two new top-of-the-line fishing rods. Slim patted him on the shoulder and whispered, "Paybacks are so painful."

In the afternoon, when Slim made it back to his house, the first thing he did was check the rain gauge. Then he pounced on the telephone and called Chief Deputy Kile. "Hey Bobby, how much rain did you get?"

"It was a nice rain, three-quarters of an inch."

"*Three and a half inches, buddy, so chew on that!*" He slammed down the phone and actually danced around the room, the happiest cowboy in the whole Texas Panhandle.

And that's about all the…wait, there was one last thing. When Sally May got all her things moved back into the house from the trip, the first thing she did, I mean the *first* thing…she went straight to the freezer compartment of the refrigerator and checked on the ice cream.

They got caught, nailed.

I could have told them. She has radar for naughty behavior and for once, she'd caught someone besides ME! I loved it.

And that's the story of the Lost Camp. This case is closed.

Have you read all of Hank's adventures?

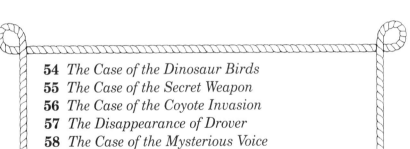

Finding Hank

The Most-Often Asked Questions about Hank the Cowdog

For more than 35 years, John R. Erickson has entertained three generations of readers with Hank the Cowdog's hilarious antics, and now, for the first time, in this beautiful, full-color volume, he answers the most common questions he has received from fans over the years!

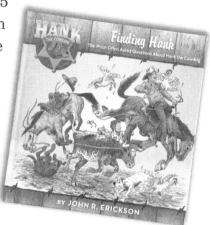

Written in an engaging question-and-answer style, this collector's item — complete with illustrations and original photographs — provides a unique behind-the-scenes look at the people, places, and real-life animals and incidents behind your favorite Hank stories!

And, be sure to check out the
Audiobooks!

If you've never heard a *Hank the Cowdog* audiobook, you're missing out on a lot of fun! Each Hank book has also been recorded as an unabridged audiobook for the whole family to enjoy!

Praise for the Hank Audiobooks:

"It's about time the Lone Star State stopped hogging Hank the Cowdog, the hilarious adventure series about a crime solving ranch dog. Ostensibly for children, the audio renditions by author John R. Erickson are sure to build a cult following among adults as well." *— Parade Magazine*

"Full of regional humor . . . vocals are suitably poignant and ridiculous. A wonderful yarn." *— Booklist*

"For the detectin' and protectin' exploits of the canine Mike Hammer, hang Hank's name right up there with those of other anthropomorphic greats...But there's no sentimentality in Hank: he's just plain more rip-roaring fun than the others. Hank's misadventures as head of ranch security on a spread somewhere in the Texas Panhandle are marvelous situation comedy." *— School Library Journal*

"Knee-slapping funny and gets kids reading."

— Fort Worth Star Telegram

The Ranch Life Learning Series

Want to learn more about ranching? Check out Hank's hilarious and educational new series, Ranch Life Learning, brought to you by Maverick Books and The National Ranching Heritage Center!

Saddle up for some fun as the same cast of characters you've come to know and love in the Hank the Cowdog series gives you a first-class introduction to life on a ranch!

In these books, you'll learn things like: the difference between a ranch and a farm, how cows digest grass, what it takes to run a ranch as a successful business, how to take care of cattle throughout the various seasons, what the daily life of a working cowboy looks like, qualities to look for in a good horse, the many kinds of wild animals you might see if you spent a few days on Hank's ranch, the tremendous impact different kinds of weather have on every aspect of ranching, and much, much more!

Hold on to your saddles!
Winter 2021:

The National Ranching Heritage Center and Hank the Cowdog are proud to partner once again for *Prairie Fires,* the fifth book in the Ranch Life Learning series. You may not have known it, but Hank's job as Head of Ranch Security includes another very important role: Fire Marshall. With Hank as your guide, you'll learn about how prairie fires get started, how to fight them and how to prevent them.

Moreover, Hank will explain the distinct characteristics of *wildfires* and how they must be fought differently than your typical prairie fires. Drawing from his own experience with a wildfire that hit the ranch, Hank explains the after-effects of fire, including its devastating consequences and some very surprising benefits!

Love Hank's Hilarious Songs?

Hank the Cowdog's "Greatest Hits" albums bring together the music from the unabridged audiobooks you know and love! These wonderful collections of hilarious (and sometimes touching) songs are unmatched. Where else can you learn about coyote philosophy, buzzard lore, why your dog is protecting an old corncob, how bugs compare to hot dog buns, and much more!

And, be sure to visit Hank's "Music Page" on the official website to listen to some of the songs and download FREE Hank the Cowdog ringtones!

"Audio-Only" Stories

Ever wondered what those "Audio-Only" Stories in Hank's Official Store are all about?

The Audio-Only Stories are Hank the Cowdog adventures that have never been released as books. They are about half the length of a typical Hank book, and there are currently seven of them. They have run as serial stories in newspapers for years and are now available as audiobooks!

Have you visited Hank's official website yet?

www.hankthecowdog.com

Don't miss out on exciting *Hank the Cowdog* games and activities, as well as up-to-date news about upcoming books in the series!

When you visit, you'll find:

- Hank's BLOG, which is the first place we announce upcoming books and new products!
- Hank's Official Shop, with tons of great *Hank the Cowdog* books, audiobooks, games, t-shirts, stuffed animals, mugs, bags, and more!
- Links to Hank's social media, whereby Hank sends out his "Cowdog Wisdom" to fans.
- A FREE, printable "Map of Hank's Ranch"!
- Hank's Music Page where you can listen to songs and even download FREE ringtones!
- A way to sign up for Hank's free email updates
- Sally May's "Ranch Roundup Recipes"!
- Printable & Colorable Greeting Cards for Holidays.

- Articles about Hank and author John R. Erickson in the news,

...AND MUCH, MUCH MORE!

BOOKS
The Collection

FAN ZONE
Fun & Games

AUTHOR
Meet the Creator

STORE
Books & More

ANNOUNCING:
A sneak peek
at Hank #66

Ever thought of having a
Hank the Cowdog Stuffed Party!

Hank Plays Cupid:

Find Toys, Games, Books & More
at the Hank shop.

GAMES
COME PLAY WITH
HANK & PALS

BOOKS
BROWSE THE ENTIRE
HANK CATALOG

FRIENDS
GET TO KNOW THE
RANCH GANG

Visit Hank's
Facebook
page

Follow Hank
on Twitter

Watch Hank
on YouTube

Follow Hank
on Pinterest

Send Hank
an Email

FROM THE BLOG

JAN 26 Hank is Cupid in Disguise...

JAN 18 The Valentine's Day Robbery! - a Snippet from the Story

DEC 04 Getting SIGNED Hank the Cowdog books for Christmas!

OCT 16 Education Association's lists of recommended books?

[VISIT THE BLOG]

Hank's Music.
Free ringtones,
music and more!

[MORE]

Hank's Survey
We'd love to know what you think! [GO]

Official Shop
Find books, audio,
toys and more!

[LET'S GO]

Get the Latest
Keep up with Hank's news
and promotions by signing
up for our e-news.

Looking for The Hank Times
fan club newsletter?

[Enter your email address]
[SIGN UP]

TEACHER'S CORNER
Download fun activity guides,
discussion questions and more.

Join Hank's Security Force
Get the activity letter and
other cool stuff.

[JOIN] SECURITY FORCE

SALLY MAY'S RECIPES

Discover delicious recipes from
Sally May herself. [GO]

Hank in the News
Find out what the media
is saying about Hank. [GO]

FEATURED BOOK

The Christmas Turkey Disaster

Now Available!
Hank is in real trouble this time. L...

[BUY] [READ] [LISTEN]

BOOKS
Browse Titles
Buy Books
Audio Samples
Other Books

FAN ZONE
Games
Hank & Friends
Security Force
Educational Stuff

AUTHOR
John Erickson's Bio
Hank in the News
In Concert
Contact John

SHOP
The Books
Store
Get Help
Retailer Info

Teacher's Corner

Know a teacher who uses Hank in their class-room? You'll want to be sure they know about Hank's "Teacher's Corner"! Just click on the link on the homepage, and you'll find free teacher's aids, such as a printable map of Hank's ranch, a reading log, coloring pages, blog posts specifically for teachers and librarians, quizzes and much more!

The Very Best Toy

by Gary Rinker

A Picture Book for Young Readers

What is the very best toy? Playing with Dad! Through a child's imagination, a dad becomes a swing, a horse, a slide, a trampoline and more!

Mom's Choice Award Winner!

Best Books 2011 Award Winner in Children's Picture Book from USA News

Collect the Entire Series!

Have you visited the "Set and Combo Packs" page in Hank's Store? Check out our deals on two-packs and bundles, as well as a special discount for buying the entire series at one time!

Join Hank the Cowdog's Security Force

Are you a big Hank the Cowdog fan? Then you'll want to join Hank's Security Force. Here is some of the neat stuff you will receive:

Welcome Package
- A Hank paperback of your choice
- An original Hank poster (19" x 25")
- A Hank bookmark

Eight digital issues of *The Hank Times* newspaper with

- Lots of great games and puzzles
- Stories about Hank and his friends
- Special previews of future books
- Fun contests

More Security Force Benefits
- Special discounts on Hank books, audios, and more
- Special Members Only section on Hank's website at www.hankthecowdog.com

Total value of the Welcome Package and *The Hank Times* is $23.99. However, your two-year membership is **only $7.99** plus $5.00 for shipping and handling.

- -

☐ Yes, I want to join Hank's Security Force. Enclosed is $12.99 ($7.99 + $5.00 for shipping and handling) for my **two-year membership**. [Make check payable to Maverick Books. International shipping extra.]

WHICH BOOK WOULD YOU LIKE TO RECEIVE IN YOUR WELCOME PACKAGE? CHOOSE ANY BOOK IN THE SERIES. (EXCEPT #50) (#)

	BOY or GIRL
YOUR NAME	(CIRCLE ONE)

MAILING ADDRESS

CITY	STATE	ZIP

TELEPHONE	BIRTH DATE

E-MAIL   (REQUIRED FOR DIGITAL HANK TIMES)

Send check or money order for $12.99 to:

Hank's Security Force
Maverick Books
P.O. Box 549
Perryton, Texas 79070
Offer is subject to change

DO NOT SEND CASH.   NO CREDIT CARDS ACCEPTED.
ALLOW 2-3 WEEKS FOR DELIVERY

The following activities are samples from *The Hank Times*, the official newspaper of Hank's Security Force. Please do not write on these pages unless this is your book. And, even then, why not just find a scrap of paper?

"Photogenic"
Memory Quiz

We all know that Hank has a "photogenic" memory—being aware of your surroundings is an important quality for a Head of Ranch Security. Now *you* can test your powers of observation.

How good is your memory? Look at the illustration on page 35 and try to remember as many things about it as possible. Then turn back to this page and see how many questions you can answer.

1. How many birds were there? 1, 2, 3, or 4?

2. Which of HANK'S eyes could you see?
HIS Left or Right?

3. How many trees were there? 1, 2, 3, or 4?

4. Could you see Drover's tail? Yes or No?

5. How many of Drover's ears
could you see? 1, 2, 3,
or all 4?

"Rhyme Time"

When Little Alfred grows up, what kinds of jobs do you think he'll consider? Make a rhyme using "Alfred" that would relate to his new job possibilities.

Example: Alfred becomes a school crosswalk guard.

Answer: Alfred **RED.**

1. Alfred supplies sleeping bags to a camping supply store.

2. Alfred starts a dog food company.

3. Alfred makes store mannequins to display cowboy hats.

4. Alfred gets a job as an audiobook performer.

5. Alfred gets famous and becomes one of the most quotable people.

6. Alfred becomes a preacher and opens a chapel to marry couples.

7. Alfred builds this type of lawn-mower storage units.

8. Alfred works as a museum tour guide.

"Photogenic"
Memory Quiz

W̲e all know that Hank has a "photogenic" memory—being aware of your surroundings is an important quality for a Head of Ranch Security. Now *you* can test your powers of observation.

How good is your memory? Look at the illustration on page 72 and try to remember as many things about it as possible. Then turn back to this page and see how many questions you can answer.

1. How many barbed wire strands are above the fence? 1, 2, or 3?

2. Was Loper's belt buckle: Square, Round, Rectangle or Oval-shaped?

3. Which of LOPER'S hands was higher? HIS Left or Right?

4. How many pockets were on Loper's shirt? 1, 2, or "What Pockets"?

5. How many of Loper's eyes could you see? 1, 2, 3, or all 4?

"Word Maker"

Try making up to twenty words from the letters in the names below. Use as many letters as possible, however, don't just add an "s" to a word you've already listed in order to have it count as another. Try to make up entirely new words for each line!

Then, count the total number of letters used in all of the words you made, and see how well you did using the Security Force Rankings below!

W O O D R O W   S L I M

_____   _____

_____   _____

_____   _____

_____   _____

_____   _____

_____   _____

_____   _____

_____   _____

_____   _____

_____   _____

55 - 61 You spend too much time with J.T. Cluck and the chickens.

62 - 65 You are showing some real Security Force potential.

66 - 69 You have earned a spot on our Ranch Security team.

70 +   Wow! You rank up there as a top-of-the-line cowdog.

John R. Erickson, a former cowboy, has written numerous books for both children and adults and is best known for his acclaimed *Hank the Cowdog* series. The *Hank* series began as a self-publishing venture in Erickson's garage in 1982 and has endured to become one of the nation's most popular series for children and families.

Through the eyes of Hank the Cowdog, a smelly, smart-aleck Head of Ranch Security, Erickson gives readers a glimpse into daily life on a cattle ranch in the West Texas Panhandle. His stories have won a number of awards, including the Audie, Oppenheimer, Wrangler, and Lamplighter Awards, and have been translated into Spanish, Danish, Farsi, and Chinese. In 2019, Erickson was inducted into the Texas Literary Hall of Fame. *USA Today* calls the *Hank the Cowdog* books "the best family entertainment in years." Erickson lives and works on his ranch in Perryton, Texas, with his family.

Nicolette G. Earley

was born and raised in the Texas Hill Country. She began working for Maverick Books in 2008, editing, designing new Hank the Cowdog books, and working with the artist who had put faces on all the characters: Gerald Holmes. When Holmes died in 2019, she discovered that she could reproduce his drawing style and auditioned for the job. She made her debut appearance in Book 75, illustrating new books in the series she read as a child. She and her husband, Keith, now live in coastal Mississippi.